LEGEND OF HELL

CHRISTOPHER ALLEN

Copyright © 2021 by Christopher Allen

All rights reserved. No part of this publication may be reproduced, distributed, or transmitted in any form or by any means, including photocopying, recording, or other electronic or mechanical methods, without the prior written permission of the publisher, except in the case brief quotations embodied in critical reviews and other noncommercial uses permitted by copyright law.

ISBN: 978-1-63945-263-7 (Paperback)
    978-1-63945-264-4 (E-book)

The views expressed in this book are solely those of the author and do not necessarily reflect the views of the publisher, and the publisher hereby disclaims any responsibility for them.

Writers' Branding
1800-608-6550
www.writersbranding.com
orders@writersbranding.com

Contents

Year 1: Car Accident · · · · · · · · · · · · · · · · · ·1
A Four-Year Journey · · · · · · · · · · · · · · · · ·9
Purgatory & the Great Desert · · · · · · · · · 13
Limbo · 21
Lake of Fire & Tukuk · · · · · · · · · · · · · · · · 27
Tower of Babel· 31
Year 2: Ziz & the Power · · · · · · · · · · · · · · 41
Sacred Prostitution· · · · · · · · · · · · · · · · · · 57
The Forest of Aokigahara· · · · · · · · · · · · · 71
Mammon, Prince of Hell· · · · · · · · · · · · · 79
Behemoth· 83
Hammer of the Damned · · · · · · · · · · · · · 89
Year 3: Cain & The Sword
 of Damascus · 97
Azazel, the Angel of Death · · · · · · · · · · 105
Baal & Leviathan · · · · · · · · · · · · · · · · · · 111
Sheol & Astaroth · · · · · · · · · · · · · · · · · · 121
Year 4:
Frozen wasteland of Gehenna· · · · · · · · · 139
Ending: The Coming War · · · · · · · · · · · 151

Year 1: Car Accident

Well, where do I begin…I guess if you don't think I'm crazy, I'll start at the beginning four years ago on the rainy night that changed my life forever. The night I went to hell…yes, the place with fire. And the evil demons aren't all bad, just a little crazy for this world. So all I ask is that you keep a clear head about this and remember, I know a little more about everything than you do.

It just started to rain, and in my mind, I had about half an hour until it really started to rain, so I thought I was good. I was going to meet my family about two hours away in Rocky Mount, North Carolina, and I was having a good time too. I had just looked down to change the station on the radio, and from the corner of my eye, I thought I saw something cross the road and looked up to see nothing. "Take it easy, Freddie, you just got started. You can't get crazy just yet," I said to myself. Then, I saw a sign that would take me off to State Road 301 that would have taken me back way into Rocky Mount, so I took it hoping for a change of pace than just the same old way every time. I came off the ramp onto the 301 and saw that the light along the road was very little, and at some point, I had to use the high beams when things got a little weird.

First, was the radio going in and out, weird because the station was in Wilson, about twenty minutes away from where I was. Then came the car…the lights were next to go, and like the radio, they went out for about a whole five minutes. By the time they came on, there's this woman on the road. She had a scared look on her face. So I turned the wheel hard to the left and went right in the ditch. The front-end stopped, and the car was up in the air, crashing hard onto the ground, and that's when I blacked out.

"Wake up, human…." a voice said as my eyes opened to an open field to my left. "Well, this is a surprise. Humans don't come to me and not to my doorstep," the voice said. I looked over and saw a man standing over me. "Hello, sir…I think I crashed my car," I said, standing up. "Yes, you did, but you're not supposed to be here," the man said, helping me to stand up straight. "What do you mean, here? I mean, where are we?" I questioned. "Hell boy, but you're not dead. So I could ask you the same question," the man said. "Hell…?" I asked, looking around. "Don't worry, the fire and tearing of souls isn't here," the man said. "Sorry, I'm Jophiel. Keeper of this place and archangel," he said. "No…this can't be right…I never did anything bad," I said. "Well, let's start with names first," Jophiel said, holding out his hand. "Fred…Freddie," I stuttered. "Good, nice to meet you, Freddie, and yes, from what I'm getting from you, you're not supposed to be here either," Jophiel said with a smile. "What do you mean by that?" I asked. "Well, first off, your soul came to my house, which has never happened before…meaning you're going to do something here that will change things," Jophiel answered. "In hell…?" I questioned. "Come, we can talk about it inside. This place might be safe at first glance, but don't be deceived. Come this way," Jophiel said, showing me to the door. We walked into a large house sitting to the right of us. I looked up to the sky and saw a tower in the distance that reached the red sky. "Yes, that is the Tower of Babel…a bad place for you to go," Jophiel said, walking into the house. "So, I'm in hell…." I said, looking over at him. "Well…yes and no, this place was made for humans that didn't take in the word of the Creator. Who you would call God, but these souls still did good in their lifetime, so they come here," Jophiel said as we entered the house, he pointed to a group of chairs sitting around a small table. "Has anything like this ever happened before?" I asked. "Well, not like this. You still have your human body… you see?" Jophiel said, poking my hand. "Ouch…." I said, rubbing my hand. "See, human body…that's never happened before, and even if it did, you should have someone with you…like a guide," Jophiel said. "Great, I'm in hell, and there's no way out," I said. "There is a way out but getting there is the problem," Jophiel said. "The way out is in the frozen hell known as Gehenna. To get there is about four years long," Jophiel added. "Four years...?!" I shouted. "Yes, but I want to talk to the others and see what is going on. Why is there a human in hell still with his body?" Jophiel said, pointing a long horn out the window. He blew into it with a force that I have never seen before, "There, we should have them soon," Jophiel said, handing me a glass of water. "Should I take that?" I asked. "Yes, but this water will last you about a month once you drink it," Jophiel said. "What? That's impossible," I laughed, looking at the cup. "Well, you're the one in hell talking to an angel...nothing is impossible anymore," Jophiel said. I looked at him and smiled a little. *I just wanted to go home and be with my grandpa and friends*, in the back of my mind. *Now I'm in hell, and it might take me four years to get back home.* "Don't worry, Freddie...if we can get you back home, then we will try our best," Jophiel said, trying to cheer me up. "Thank you," I said, looking out the window to see five beams of light fill the sky. "What is that?" I asked, pointing out the window. "My friends, Freddie," Jophiel said as four men and a woman stood at the back window. "Whoa... now I'm not worried," I said. "Brother Jophiel, what is going on here?" one of the men said, walking up the window. "We have an odd problem that I need some help with. Here, I like you to meet Freddie, a human from the Creator's world," Jophiel said, pointing to me. I stood there blankly, waving at them, "Impossible...a human with his body...here?" the man said. "Weirder things have happened in the place," the woman said, stepping to the window. "Come in, brothers and sister. We must try to send him back to the world," Jophiel said.

Once the angels were inside, and they were told about my story, they talked to Jophiel before turning to me, and from what I could tell, this was not going to be an easy fix. "Freddie, we can't send you back... not with our power," the woman said. She was known as Uriel. A fine-looking woman if you ask me. "We might be able to take him the hole," the man said, walking over to me. This guy was known as Gabriel and, from what I heard, a real badass. "He's a human with a human body. If we can get him there, it would only be through the grace of the Creator," the other man said, sitting down next to me. This guy was Raphael and sounded like an angel that played it safe for most of his life. "Wait...what is the hole?" I asked. "The hole is how demons here enter the Creator's world. They have only one rule. They must not kill you by their own hand," Gabriel said. "That's it? Sound like a good rule to me," I said. "Okay, this hole will take me home, and that's it?" I added. "Yes, but you must realize that it will take you four years to get there once we start, or worse, the demons will try to kill you," Jophiel said, looking over to me. "Great, so this will take a long time, and I might die. My grandpa always said that nothing in life is free," I said. "Your grandpa must be a wise man in the Creator's world," Uriel said. "No, just old," I said with a small smile on my face. "Then we must get you ready to go. I will start with you," Jophiel said. "Wait, what about the rest of you?" I questioned. "They can smell us, and in a large group, we would hurt your chances of returning home," Gabriel answered. "So, taking a turn, I see. So you don't get sick of the human. I got it," I said. I felt like that homeless man that asks for money and gets nothing every time I ask. "Don't worry if this works. You will be the only human that will know about and has ever seen an angel," Jophiel said. "Sounds good…I guess," I said. "But first, we will take you to the door," Uriel said. "The door…there's no way he can open it," Michael said, looking over to me. "Wait…what door?" I asked, looking at them.

    Ask a stupid question, get a foolish answer…I was now standing before a door, the kind you might see in a medieval movie. The angels stood behind me. The only ones that walked up to it with me were Jophiel and Uriel. "So, what will this prove that I'm a fish out of water? Or in this case, a human in hell?" I murmured. "I think you might be the person that we're waiting for," Jophiel said. "But they don't believe me…." Jophiel added. "I'll try not to let you down then," I said, walking over to the door. It looked metal and had a funny-looking symbol on it that I never saw before. Think of a star, put two verticals on both sides, and that's what it was. "Listen…I'm an engineer, so I have to ask will this door blow up or kill me in some way?" I asked. "No, Freddie, you must trust us, my friend," Michael answered. *Yeah, sure then, why are four of you standing way back?* I said to myself. I put my hand on the door and pushed it open, and closed my eyes just in case. Jophiel and Uriel touched my shoulders on both sides, "Well done," Jophiel said. I opened my eyes, and there it was. Total darkness. "The door doesn't go anywhere," I said. Both Jophiel and Uriel didn't let go of my shoulders yet like if I would fly off at that point. "Where does it go?" I asked. "I don't know...it's your door," Uriel said. "Good, Freddie can enter the door later, and one of us will go with him," Michael said. I was about to ask a question when my stomach made the dinner bell sound, and all the angels turned to me with weird looks on their faces. "What was that?" Uriel asked, poking my stomach. "I'm hungry...how long has it been?" I question back. "About a day so far," Jophiel answered. "What? It hasn't gotten dark yet?" I said. "Oh, sorry, should have told you that there's no sun here, so it's never dark in hell," Jophiel said. "Thanks...." I murmured. "This way, I'll see if I can find you some food," Jophiel said, walking back to the house.

Jophiel was good at cooking...either that or whatever the hell I was eating. It tasted excellent. He didn't tell me what it was just as long as it wasn't roadkill, I guess. Uriel was sitting beside me, and I couldn't shake the feeling that she was someone I knew; I just couldn't place the face. Uriel had red-colored hair that fit well with her blue eyes, and she wasn't a bad looker either. I know what you're saying, Freddie Johnson, you're going to hell for that...news flash already in agony, so I can't do much worst than that. The other angels were still looking at the door I opened a while ago, and now we're talking about it. I turned to Uriel, and I saw that our eyes had met, "Tell me...what's the deal with the door?" I asked. Uriel looked over to it, then back to me before she spoke, "Freddie, you will walk through that door and face your fears, the things you hate, and the things that make you cried," Uriel answered. "Damn, sounds like an intervention," I said. Uriel looked puzzled, "What is this intervention?" She questioned. "A human thing everyone comes together and tell the person that they suck at life and you need to stop doing what you're doing," I answered. "Then this would be one of those," Uriel said. Michael walked over to us, "Freddie...are you ready?" he asked. I stood up and looked over to the door. "Jophiel will go with you to keep you safe," Michael added. "Wait...safe? What is it in there?" I asked. "Your fears and failures are through that door. If you can overcome them, then you will be ready for what you will see in there," Michael said, pointing to the tower from a distance. "Okay...I'm ready," I said, walking over to the door. Jophiel walked behind me, and I felt a little better that he was going in there with me. I approached the door and in front of me was darkness, "Ready," I said, looking back at Jophiel. "Are you?" he questioned back. *No*, I thought in my head, *but if this gets me closer to home, then fine.* I stepped thru the door and into the darkness.

I was with Jophiel standing in a living room that I didn't know at first until the yelling started. "You drink too much!" a woman's voice said. "Shut the fuck up, woman!" the man shouted, and a loud crash could be heard. I walked down the hallway and stopped when I saw a small child sitting on the bed. "I thought I already forgot about this," I said. "My stepfather was a drunk and would hit my mother," I told Jophiel as another crash made the small boy jump. "What did that make out of you?" Jophiel asked. "Angry," I answered. "I'm guessing I can't do anything about this," I added. "No, that time has passed you by," Jophiel said. "Could have done something," I said. "No, you were a child, and what could you have done?" Jophiel questioned. "Something!" I snapped. It must have surprised Jophiel. "I'm guessing you don't show emotions easily," Jophiel said. "I'm an Army guy…there not supposed to come out easy," I said. Like sand in the desert, the scene blew away, and we have left the darkness again. A glow of light was the only thing that came from Jophiel. The man had wings, real glowing wings. "Humans are emotional people, Freddie. You must go to them, and you must let them free," Jophiel said. "I don't think that can happen again," I said. "What happened to you to make you feel this way?" Jophiel asked. Just then, we were walking on grass, and a large group of people was gathering in a cemetery. Jophiel walked up, and I soon followed, but I already knew what it was, "The day I had to say bye to her for the last time," I said. I saw myself sitting next to two women as one of them was taking the flag. Almost eleven years ago since that day…I still haven't moved on, I guess. I could tell that I was crying. Two puffy brown eyes with tears running down my brown face. "I see…" Jophiel said, looking over at me. "The death of this woman was not your fault, Freddie Johnson," Jophiel said. "Then why do I feel like this?" I said, and a tear ran down my face as I looked over to him. "Because you loved her…I ask you to love something more than yourself again," Jophiel answered. I wiped the tear from my face as the scene disappeared like smoke off a cigar. Jophiel's light was once again the only one in the darkness. Jophiel stopped and looked over to the left. I looked over to see another scene. This one was that of a dirt road lying. In the middle of this was a man dressed in Army Combat Uniform. "I hate to ask Freddie, but who is this?" Jophiel asked. "One of my friends...Roy Carlton," I answered. "I'm sorry, my friend," he said. "We did a great job...I guess," I said. "This happens in the world there?" Jophiel questioned. "Yes, mostly for country...not sure God wouldn't approve of all this killing," I answered. "The Creator wouldn't approve of this, but then again, we haven't been to that world in some time," Jophiel said. "Looks like we're back," Jophiel added. I looked over to see the opened door and the angels standing there. "Good, can't take much more crying," I said with a smile. "Wait, there is something you need to see," Jophiel said. In his hands was a small ball of light that he held out to me. "What's this?" I asked. "An angel's name means more than just a name. Take this light, and you will have courage, bravery, and valor of the Creator," Jophiel answered. "So, your name stands for courage then?" I questioned. "Yes, the courage of the Creator or what you humans would call...one with great courage," Jophiel answered, handing me the ball of light. I took it from him, and the ball of light slowly disappeared into my hands. I stood there for a moment. "I don't feel any different," I said. "Don't worry, Freddie. Courage is not something you can see. It's like faith. When you need it, it will be there. Don't worry," Jophiel said as we walked to the door. I stepped out, and the angels walked over to us, "So he gained what he needed for the journey?" Michael asked. "Yes, he is ready to leave at any time," Jophiel answered. "If it's okay with you, we can leave once we get a few things," Michael said. "In the meantime, Gabriel will tell you what you will be dealing with out there," Michael added.

A Four-Year Journey

Gabriel sat under the only tree next to the house. He had a piece of paper in his hands when I walked up. "Freddie, I heard you got Jophiel's courage. You will need it for the journey," Gabriel said. Gabriel was the tallest out of the angel, about six feet, eight inches, with short black hair and a tan by human standards. He was dressed like he was ready for a walk in the hardest part of a city with a chain that held something in his pocket to match his black hair with jeans and a red long sleeve shirt. "I didn't think angels would wear stuff like this," I said, pointing to the shirt. "There is always a first time for everything...like you humans say," Gabriel said, pointing to a map sitting on the ground. "This will be a long journey, and it will take us through the five lands of hell and into the very coldest part of hell and the hottest," Gabriel added. "So, what's our first stop?" I asked. "First, we will have to cross the desert of Purgatory. From there, the Limbo and the Forest of Suicide are known as Aokigahara. After that, Sheol, and last Gehenna, the coldest part of hell. Where one of the five Princes of Hell is being held as prisoners," Gabriel answered. "Okay, first question, who are these Princes of Hell, and should we be worried about them?" I questioned. "We don't have to worry about them. The Fallen Angels have overthrown them and are taking over," Gabriel answered. "Fallen Angels...I have a feeling that's bad," I murmured. "Yes, that is...bad," Gabriel said. "What's the bad part about this?" I asked. Gabriel looked over at me, "Fallen Angels cared nothing about humans and questioned the Creator about the love we gave to you humans. They are mostly in Limbo, Gehenna, and Sheol. Unlike the demons that live in hell, these angels can feel us and can find us. Which is why only one of us can go with you at a time," Gabriel answered. "I see…that makes sense," I said. "Don't worry, Jophiel is going to see if a Throne can watch over you if anyone of us falls," Gabriel said. "What's a…Throne?" I questioned. "Its power comes from the Creator himself. Once you see one, you will know that the Creator is true," Gabriel answered. "First, will have to past the Wall of the Watchers then will be in hell," Gabriel added. "Wall of the Watcher?" I repeated. "Don't worry, it all will be clear once we get there," Gabriel said. *I wish I knew more about this, but the more I ask, the more confused I come*, I thought. "So when do we leave?" I asked. "Once Jophiel is ready," Gabriel answered. I looked around to see Jophiel and Michael on one knee. "Are they praying?" I asked. "Yes, they're trying to get a Throne. It's no easy task. They must pray to Creator. From there, it's up to the Powers," Gabriel answered. I didn't ask a question because it would mean that I would be more confused than I already am. I sat down and waited, looking up at the red sky that never changed. *How long have I been here, and what is going on back where I was?* These questions entered my mind like a fog and hung around a little too long for my taste. If you were asking me. Jophiel and Michael stood up and were talking again before Jophiel came over to me. "Are you ready?" Jophiel asked. "As ready as I'll ever be," I answered. I should've been scared, but I wasn't wondering what is in hell and leaving this joker with any luck. "Here, hold on to this," Jophiel said, handing me a bag. "Is there like some kind of weapon in here?" I whispered. "Food Freddie…no weapons," Jophiel said with a smile. I haven't left his house yet, and I just made myself look stupid…*good job, Johnson*. Jophiel started to walk off, and I followed, crossing the open field with people walking around. To me, they looked like they were walking around in a dazing. "Jophiel, I feel kind of stupid asking you but are these people's souls?" I asked. "Yes, these are people that lived their life good but didn't believe in the word of the Creator, so they are here," Jophiel answered. One soul walked by me, and you couldn't tell that it wasn't a person until you looked at their faces. Their eyes were black as charcoal, and they were missing lips. "I see…that's new," I said. "It's not as bad as you think. These souls are reliving the happiest moments of their lives," Jophiel said. "That's as good as it's going to get, I guess," I said. By this time, the house was off in the distance, and a forest was coming up. "Here we go," I murmured.

Michael watched as they disappeared into the forest and looked over to Raphael and Uriel. "Did anyone else sense that part of that human was angelic?" Michael questioned. "Little, but not much…could be more to him than what appears," Raphael answered. "Maybe, but… there was a little demon in him as well," Michael said. "Impossible…." Uriel murmured. "Impossible? There is a human in hell, so impossible is not a good word to use now," Michael said.

From what I was told for Jophiel, the Wall of the Watchers was just past the forest. From there, we would pass into hell. A long walk and a whole lot of bitching would start. "So who are the Watchers…good guys, I hope?" I asked. "They are the Creator's first line of defense for the souls in the Field," Jophiel answered. "What do they look like?" I asked. "You can find out for yourself. We're here," Jophiel answered, pointing up the wall that disappeared in a weird fog that was thick. "Where are the Watchers?" I questioned. "They're here," Jophiel said. Just then, a pair of wings appeared, and…well, it was an owl.

A really big fucking owl…I'm talking like a thirty-story building, but what got me were its eyes. Big and black with a silver ring inside them, even the courage I gained from Jophiel was almost screaming at me that this owl was not to be fucked with. "Wow, that's a big owl. I murmured. "A big what?" Jophiel questioned back. "On Earth, there are animals just like this, but they're smaller, called owls," I answered. "Well, possibly, that is where most of the Watchers are based. On animals of the Creator's world," Jophiel said. "Hot damn…that's a big ass owl," I murmured. "You said that twice…the Watchers won't hurt you," Jophiel said. *I see, so why they called them Watchers?* From the moment we started walking to the wall, they were watching us. I looked over to see the same big owl-like bird next to him and the same going down the line. "How many of them are there?" I asked. "They line hell, so about a million," Jophiel answered. "Damn…bird watcher would have a field day with this place," I said. "Okay, Freddie, just past this wall is the Purgatory which is nothing but a vast desert. From here on, use my courage. The things in Purgatory would cause you to kill yourself or another, so keep your wit with you, Freddie," Jophiel said. *Okay, thanks for telling me this now*, I thought. As we passed through a small door at the bottom of one of the Watchers. "Well, here goes nothing," I murmured and stepped through the door. The smell was the first thing that hit you like a truck. "What's that smell?!" I coughed. "Hellfire and brimstone…human. You had never smelled this before?" Jophiel asked. "I see, not a good vacation spot," I said. "You haven't seen anything yet?" Jophiel said as we walked down the small hill to the flat land. I looked back and saw the Watchers, and most of them are watching back at us.

Purgatory & the Great Desert

We walked for a little after the hill and saw a man walking, but it looked like he was having trouble. "What's up with him?" I asked. Jophiel looked over and stopped. "Be careful…he is pulling his sin behind him," Jophiel answered. "There is something you must know. Stay away from the souls here. If they get close to you, they can pass their sin off to you, and I only know of one way to get it off," Jophiel added. "Okay, got it," I said. The wind started to blow, the sand hit my body, and my skin almost instantly started to burn. "What the hell is going on?!" I shouted. Jophiel's wings suddenly appeared and covered me with them. "I don't think this should happen," Jophiel said. Whatever is in the sand, it's burning hot. I tried to cover my face to protect it from getting burnt. "Come, this way," he said, pulling me along. I couldn't see anything, and my eyes hurt. The only way I made was the courage I got from Jophiel, and even then, I could feel it slowly going away until I blacked out.

Jophiel carried me. The human weight was close to nothing, and he had to get me inside to heal me. My skin was burned already, and he could smell it as he carried me on. "This will only get worse, and he might die if this wind keeps blowing," Jophiel said. Just then, at the top of a hill, he saw what looked like a cave. "Hang on, Freddie, your saving grace is here," he murmured. I already looked terrible. He would have to break one of the rules to get me there. He straight up his wings and hope that the fallen ones wouldn't sense him, but that was a chance that he had to risk. He rose into the air, flew to the cave, landed just outside, and walked me quickly inside. He immediately checked my body, and it was in bad shape. I'll be lucky if I make it to the Limbo, alone out of the desert. He pulled out some rags from my bag and wrapped them around my head, arms, and legs. My body was mainly burned as he tried to save what was left.

    I woke up to Jophiel sitting next to me. I could barely move, and little moving could do was painful. "Easy, Freddie, you need to rest," Jophiel said, touching my chest. I looked over at my arms and hands. They have severely burnt with black skin around. I had cloth wrapped around most of my body, and the parts covered in the white fabric were glowing and healing back. I might have looked like a burned bread than a person. "What happened?" I questioned. "I found this cave for us to stay in for the time being," Jophiel answered. "No, I mean with my skin burning off," I asked. "Brimstone," Jophiel said. "What is that stuff? Pretty nasty on the skin," I answered, trying the smile. That just gave me more pain, "The brimstone burned your skin and almost killed you today. My mistake," Jophiel said. "I should have done this before we left, but you getting the courage was more important for you to make this trip," Jophiel added. "Looks like we might be stuck here for a while. Is there anything you can do?" I asked. "I've wrapped most of your body in Holy Cloth, so you should heal soon. If you keep the wraps on, it will give you some protection against the brimstone, but we will need to do something about this before we get to the Limbo," Jophiel answered. "Can you call anyone for help?" I questioned. "No, but someone might do something if we go there quickly," Jophiel answered. "Who?" I asked. "There's a demon power that can help not too far away in the Lake of Fire," Jophiel answered. "What?!" I said, trying to look over to him, but pain shut down my back this time. It felt like I was on fire again. "There's a demon named Tukuk. From what I was told, he was the strongest demon that ever walked here," Jophiel explained. "And?" I asked. "Tukuk was made long ago when the human race was still young. Tukuk was hell itself," Jophiel answered. I was puzzled about how a demon could help us, but I don't want to question an angel. "It was said that his body was virtually indestructible," Jophiel said. "Like Superman," I said. "Yes, if this Superman is indestructible," Jophiel said with a puzzled look on his face. "I'm guessing he wasn't your everyday demon," I said. Jophiel smiled. "Tukuk was indestructible to such that even the Creator couldn't get rid of him," Jophiel said. I must have had a puzzled look on my charred face that Jophiel could see. "But the Creator made everything, so He should be able to destroy him, right?" I questioned. "Think of Tukuk as space within a space. His body was used to house the evil souls. So when the Creator made this place, Tukuk was allowed to stay here. When he died, his sons laid him to rest in the Lake of Fire," Jophiel said. "You think Tukuk's sons will let me have that power?" I asked. "We'll see," Jophiel answered. "I fear our journey will be a hard one," Jophiel said. "Why?" I asked. "I had to fly us to this cave. Now the fallen ones know that I'm here, and they definitely want to fight," Jophiel answered. "Are they evil angels or just a group of guys that you call the fallen ones?" I asked. "They're the ones who don't want to love humans at all when the Creator told us to love you more than anything. They were so mad. Some of them tried to kill humans and became good at it," Jophiel said. Great. *It's not yet even a week, and I already have to deal with this,* I thought. "Let's hope they don't catch up with us," I said. Jophiel gave a weak smile before looking out into the desert. "Can you move?" Jophiel asked. "Barely," I answered, hoping that the fallen guys won't notice us.

An angel stood on a small cliff overlooking a large forest. From behind him came four more angels. They all sniffed the air and looked at each other. "Did you feel that power?" one asked, looking up to the angel on the cliff. "Yes, a brother is here. Michael or maybe Jophiel. I could never tell the two apart, but someone is here," the angel said, turning to the three behind. "Should we go and say "hi" to our brother?" said one of them. "No, not yet. For now, we will send our Nephilim children to bring him here, then I will peel the wings from him slowly," he said. The others laughed at this as the forest came to life and hundreds of pairs of eyes opened.

I couldn't tell how long I was lying there. The hour turned to days turned to week, but slowly my brown-colored skin returned, and the charred skin soon went away. "You're looking better, Freddie," Jophiel said. Felt better, but now I had a new problem wearing much under the holy cloth that Jophiel put on over my shirt and jeans. There wasn't much left of them. I was wearing boy shorts, and my black shirt looked like Swiss cheese. The only good thing about this was the holy cloth covering much of my body. Jophiel had pulled out something that looked like a cloak from his bag. I was envious of that bag. It was deeper than I thought. "Put that on. It should give you some protection from the brimstone," Jophiel said. "Good, as long as I don't get burned again," I said, standing to my feet. There was still pain, but not much as there was before. "Let's get going," I said. Jophiel stepped out first and looked around, seeing nothing. He waved me out, and we started up again. I took one look at the cave that knows how long we spend there before heading out into the desert. The first thing I noticed is that the cloak did its job, and with the holy cloth, I felt better than I did days ago.

Standing before the large group of eight to nine-foot-tall giants, the five angels looked out to them before one stepped forward. "My children, we have good news. A fellow brother is in hell. I want him found and brought to me. Any of my children that can find him and can bring him to me will get the pleasure to eat their flesh," the angel said. The Nephilims cheered with this thought in their mind. They marched out from the forest with blood in their eyes and murder in their hearts. "Gadreel, they might be in the great desert of Purgatory," one of the angels said. "Good, he will be easy to find," Gadreel said. "Make sure Yeqon that they find him," Gadreel said with a smile.

Getting back on our way was easy enough, but the hard part was the damn brimstone. I was ready and felt better about it as we walked. I looked up to the sky and saw the tower get closer and closer. "What is that?" I said, pointing to the tower. "Tower of Babel, built by the demons. It's ruled by Nimrod. Hopefully, you won't have to see that place," Jophiel said. "So, that's bad. I see," I whispered. We came to a large rock group, and let me tell you, these rocks looked like nothing on earth. For starters, they had a black red-like color, almost like magma, and had something like steam coming from them. "Don't get too close. That's brimstone too," Jophiel said. "Shit, what is that smell?" I asked. "Sulfur. We can go around over here," Jophiel said, pointing to a small path that cut through the rock. I heard something that sounded like thunder in the air. "What is that sound?" I asked Jophiel. "I don't hear anything, Freddie. Are you sure that you do not hear things?" Jophiel asked, turning the corner and stop suddenly. I looked past him and saw a group of souls walking like the ones I saw days ago. "We better find a way around them," Jophiel said. About five of them in total, and from the looks of it, they didn't notice us. I looked up to the sky and saw nothing. I could still hear the thunder, but I couldn't tell where it was coming from. Jophiel stepped out, and to his left, I saw a little girl appearing from the rocks. I jumped, and the girl managed to touch my arm, and a lock sound clicked. For once, I could tell people that I didn't see that coming. She just appeared from nowhere. I couldn't move anymore, and the five that were walking around looked over to us. "Shit! I got careless!" I snapped. "No, you can't look through rock," Jophiel said, looking at the chain. The chain looks like something you would see on earth, but this thing was just heavy. The weird thing was that it wasn't chained to my arm. It was chained to my soul. Jophiel hit the ground with his hand, and a wall of sandy brimstone about four feet high appeared and hit the souls, knocking them to the ground. "My light will keep them back, for now. I need to break this chain, and it will take time," Jophiel said, pulling out what looked like a lock pick and got started. I looked over Jophiel to the desert and saw something that looked like a man running, and then another. I saw at least twenty people in total and more coming over the hill. "Jophiel, what the fuck is that?" I asked, pointing to the people, primarily women running through the desert right at us. "Nephilims. Damn! they must have known that I'm here," Jophiel said, working faster. "Is there another way to get this chain off?" I asked. "Yes, but you might not like it," Jophiel answered. "These…Nephilims, what will they do if they catch us?" I questioned. "Kill you, and that might be the least that would happen," Jophiel said, trying to undo the chain. "What's the other way?" I asked, looking at him. "I could cut your soul's left arm, which would free you," Jophiel said. I looked over his shoulder and saw the wave of Nephilims, and I will tell you this I would like to stay alive if you ask me. "Cut it…we don't have time," I said. "Very well then," Jophiel said. Lightning came suddenly from the sky and hit his hand. As I cover my face, I looked back and saw a sword. It looked like an old broadsword from medieval times. The only difference was that at the end of it was an eyelet. "Ready?" Jophiel asked. "Yes!" I shouted, and Jophiel cut into my arm at the mid-forearm, and the chain dropped to the ground. I felt a pain hundred times worst than the burning skin.

It was like someone had cut me open and started taking the thing out. "Quickly, this way! The cloak has another use. Let's just hope they can't smell us," Jophiel said, running back through the path.

Gadreel was floating high in the sky above his children as flashes of lightning came down from the red sky. "Must be Jophiel. Michael would have just flown by now," he said. "We can send them in, and Jophiel won't escape us," Yeqon said with a smile. "Don't underestimate Jophiel. Most of us are down here because he outsmarted us!" Gadreel snapped. Yeqon stepped back. Gadreel looked at the line of Nephilims that ran down to the spot of the light coming from the holy cloth. "What brings you down here, brother?" Gadreel whispered to himself.

Jophiel ran back through the path and into the open. "Okay, Freddie, I'm going to need you to try and not move. Understand that the brimstone will hurt, but it's better than being eaten alive," Jophiel said. "Yeah, some burns sound a lot better than that," I said. He took the cloak off my shoulders and put it over both of us. "Lie down and remember, not a sound," Jophiel said. I laid down on the sand, and it burned, but not as much as it would have without the holy cloth. I could see my flesh smoking as footsteps made me stop breathing. I couldn't tell what was walking by, but I could care less as long as they kept moving. Jophiel looked over to me and put a finger to his lips, telling me to keep quiet. Whatever these Nephilims are, I hope they couldn't smell me. Otherwise, we might be doomed. Two stopped right in front of us as I thought we were goners if they took three more steps but stopped short and turned left, looking around a small group of rocks that we ran past. Suddenly a voice came from the sky. "What do you mean you can't find them?!" the voice said. I looked over to Jophiel, "Someone is pissed," I whispered. The smoke from my flesh started to fill the pocket, "Shit." I murmured. *This is bad*, I thought. *I will start coughing if we can get this smoke out of here.* The voice in the sky returned. "Move out! We must find them!" the voice said. Jophiel put his hand on my shoulder and pointed to the small rock group that was right in front of us. Once we were good to move, Jophiel pulled the cloak up, and we ran to the rocks as quick as we could, stopping when we got behind them. "That was a little too close for my taste," I said. "Freddie, that will be only one of many more," Jophiel said. "Who was that guy with the loud voice?"

I asked. Jophiel took his look from the sky to me then back to the sky. "Must have been Gadreel. He was once a good brother, but he spends too much time in your world and has an evil root put in him," Jophiel said, leading me through the path that went right along the edge of a vast canyon. "Holy...." I said, stopping short of walking right off into the great unknown. I must have looked funny looking thinking back on it. Most of my shirt and jeans were gone, but my boots looked like something of brick with laces coming out of them. I couldn't even call them shoes anymore. They were starting to talk, and the heel was almost gone. Jophiel stopped as the man in the sky was talking with someone else. I watched but not too much, but this angel wasn't like Jophiel and the others. First off, he looked like a hobo angel with dirty skin and black, almost evil wings that helped him float up there like Superman. Jophiel moved slowly and found a place to hide out just off the trail. "I hate to ask, but how did we make it back there?" I questioned. Jophiel looked over at me as a burning feeling started on my foot. I looked down to see that I left the bottom part of my boot at the front of the cave. "Damn," I murmured under my breath. Jophiel looked over with a small smile on his face. "Take that human shoes off, and I will wrap your feet with the holy cloth," he said. "Is that stuff like duct tape?" I asked. "What is duct tape?" Jophiel questioned back. "Nothing, I guess this isn't duct tape," I said. Whatever that stuff was, they should sell it on earth. Put band-aids out of business, that's for sure. When he wrapped my feet, he stuck his head out and waved to me to follow him. We moved a little fast this time, and we came to a stone bridge that stretches across the canyon. "We will have to move fast. I don't know if they are close behind us or not," Jophiel said. "Sounds good to me," I said, readying myself. Jophiel looked back and stepped out, and waved at me. I ran out next to him, and we both ran across the bridge. Jophiel was six paces ahead of me, but I was closing fast. We hid on the other side behind the bridge when we got across by what I would call the railing. Jophiel looked back. I watched him as he pointed to the road that was now in front of us. We ran to the top of it, and when the front cleared out, we turned back to see what Jophiel called Nephilims still walking through the desert. "They must not be the smartest tool in the shed," I said. "They might not be smart, but they make up for it in power and evil acts," Jophiel said. "So, this is Limbo?" I asked. "Yes, but first, we must go to see the President of Hell to ask if we can use the body of Tukuk," Jophiel answered. "Why just not take it?" I asked. "If you want to cross a demon of hell, then be my guess, but I'm not Gabriel," Jophiel answered. "I see your point," I murmured. I, for one, didn't need that shit either. I felt something that I didn't have for a while…I was worried. I was about to meet my first demon and look like a hobo.

Limbo

Jophiel seemed to look a little better than he was a while ago. He stopped watching the sky for the starter and looking over our shoulder, which was good, but I could feel something coming. "Who's this President of Hell you were talking about a while back?" I asked. "His name is Buer. He played a big part in hell back when the five princes were around, now he hides not out of fear but survival," Jophiel said. The brimstone under my feet changed color from black to red to more of a black gold color. "Is that gold?" I said, looking at the ground. "Yes, must be from the River of Sin," Jophiel said. "There's a gold river in hell?" I asked. "Yes, for anyone selfish or greedy in life end up in the river," Jophiel answered. "In the river, like at the bottom?" I questioned back. "Yes, you will see it soon enough. We have to travel alongside it to get to Buer and will follow it part of the way to the Lake of Fire," Jophiel answered. I start to smell something like burning trash, and to my left, I saw gold. The further we walked, the more the river came into view. "River of Sin...." I whispered to myself. Jophiel said nothing, just nodded as we walked on, but I had one question for him. "What happens to people that end up here?" I asked. Jophiel stopped walking and turned to me. "Do you really wish to know?" Jophiel questioned back. I had wished at that point that I kept my mouth shut. Jophiel walked over, and no homo held me close. "Jophiel, I need to have to talk with you about personal space," I said. "You're going to get a little of my power for a short time, so I need to get close to you. I'm sorry," Jophiel said. We stood at the edge of the river, and both of us took to our knees. "Ready?" Jophiel asked. "Okay," I answered. Still holding me close, no homo, we stuck our heads in the gold river. I opened my eyes and saw that the whole bottom of the river was covered with people. I couldn't count them all. These people's very souls were being held down by nothing but the bottom of the river. Jophiel pulled me up, and I looked over to him, "Damn! I'm guessing they got it bad," I said. Jophiel stood up. "Their souls are stuck at the bottom of that river until the end of time. They will drown every day of every hour of every second until the end of time. In some cases, the people down there have been there for five hundred years," Jophiel said. "They drown every time in their golden hell," Jophiel added. I said nothing else about that place as we walked on.

Jophiel was saying this Buer guy lives at the end of this golden river, and sure enough, I saw something that looked like a castle, and from the looks of it, it's where the gold was coming from. "We will find him here," Jophiel said. "President of Hell lives pretty nice," I said as we walked across the bridge. Jophiel looked back to see if something was following us, but I saw nothing. I just had this feeling that someone was watching and waiting for something. "Listen to me, Freddie, Buer is a demon and he doesn't like how humans think. So, just follow my lead," Jophiel said. I turned to him with a smile, "This is your chicken. I'm just holding the wing, friend," I said. I guess he understood what I was trying to say because a smile slowly came across his face.

Meanwhile, Gadreel had searched most of the desert and still couldn't find us. "How could they get around us?" Gadreel snapped. Yeqon said nothing, he has seen this many times from his brother to know that this wouldn't get past overnight. "If we head back, we could find him," Yeqon said. "Tell the others to be on the watch for the angel. Bring him to me once you find him. I wish to kill him myself," Gadreel said back. Yeqon said nothing, just nodded as Gadreel floated into the air. Just then, a Nephilim walked up to them, holding pieces of cloth. "What do you have there, my child?" Gadreel said, taking the pieces of fabric from his hand and took in a deep breath of it. "Well, human. This is nice and will make it easy to find him with a human tagging along," Gadreel murmured. He looks to the Nephilim and gave him the cloth back. "Past it around to your brothers and sisters then go at finding this angel and his human friend," Gadreel said, pointing to the desert. The tall Nephilim ran off yelling to the others. Different groups started to form. "You think this human is here to free him?" Yeqon asked. Gadreel looked over to him. "I don't know, but the Nephilims haven't had human meat in a while," Gadreel answered.

Jophiel and I walked up to a large gate that had seen a better day. Most of it was falling to the wall's right. And a skeleton of some kind was sitting up against the wall. "Something bad must have happened here," I said. "Yes, the war between the fallen and the princes of hell," Jophiel said. Jophiel pointed to the top of the wall, and some skulls and ribs littered the ground. "I thought humans had bad wars. Shit," I murmured. "Demons are like ants. If these monsters had human weapons, they all would be dead by now," Jophiel said. "I assume you've been in the human world a few times?" I asked. We had walked through the gate by now. And we're walking only by light that Jophiel made from his wings. "Yes, I have seen your power in fighting bigger than yourself, but I have also seen you fight over color, money, and revenge," Jophiel answered. He sounded almost sad when he said that. "We can be better," I countered. "True, but as a whole, and I've yet to see it," Jophiel said. We went to a large open arena that looked like hell. Bones were littered everywhere, and from what I can tell, these things were enormous. "Whose bones are those?" I asked. "Nephilims. A part of the fallen army," Jophiel answered. "Must have taken a lot of people to take this place," I said. The bones stopped in a line just before a large opening on where we were standing. "I have a feeling that standing here might be a bad idea," I whispered. "I know, but he's coming," Jophiel whispered back. Suddenly, thunderous footsteps filled the large opened arena. The bones started to move, almost like tiny ants were carrying them away. Stepping out was the weirdest shit I've ever seen. First off, this thing, if I could call it, it walked out slowly at first and stopped right in front of us. Second, it was a smash of two animals: the head of a lion and the lower body was like spider legs, but they were five goat legs that moved him along. "Damn...." I murmured. "Freddie, meet Buer, President of Hell," Jophiel said. Buer let out a mighty roar that shattered the bones around us and might have killed me if it wasn't for the holy cloth that covered my body. Jophiel's courage was the only thing keeping me from pissing my pants or what was left of them right there. I could feel that there was hate somewhere from the courage for this thing, and Jophiel must have felt the same way. "Buer, I would like to ask you to let us use the power of Tukuk…." Jophiel said until Buer cut him off with some kind of half roar half yell that made my ears hurt. "Let's take that as a no," I said. "Buer, the fallen have taken just about everything you have except your life," Jophiel said. Buer made two steps forward and was now in Jophiel's face. "I take that as a hell no then," I murmured. His hot breath smelled like a dead body, only twenty time's worst, and I could see something crawling on his skin about the size of a dollar bill. "Jophiel, may I give this a try?" I asked. Jophiel turned to me with a puzzled look on his face but took a step back as I stepped forward. Buer was a bit surprise and move to the left on his goat legs and stood up. He was about as tall as a five-story building. "From what I can tell, you need your world back, and from what I can tell, I'm the man, I mean, person for the job!" I shouted. Buer's large brown eyes looked at me with a part of puzzlement and wonder who is this tiny human that now stands in front of him. "Now I'm asking you if I can use the power Tukuk and help you get back your princes. So, what do you say?!" I asked. Buer looked down at me and gave a low roar, and stomped his goat legs into the ground. Jophiel looked over at me. "Good job, you played the game right. So now, how are you going to help him and get yourself out of here at the same time?" Jophiel questioned. "One thing at a time, friend. First Tukuk, then, I'll help him," I whispered. Buer turned and walked off his goat legs carrying him along. "Come, we must hurry and head to the Lake of Fire before the fallen catches up with us," Jophiel said. "Sounds good to me," I said, walking behind him.

  Gadreel was floating high in the sky, looking around at his army that now walked back into Limbo. "They're here somewhere, my brother. You really are good at this game," Gadreel said to himself. Gadreel had his army of children head back across the Limbo after they found a shoe by the canyon. He felt that he's already close to his brother and this human who was with him. Right now, he was waiting for the others to show up and start the search. Then, from Sheol came the other three angels. "Took you all long enough," Gadreel said. "Sorry, at first we couldn't believe that a human is here in Hell," one of the more minor angels said. "Yes, this is true, but now we're going to put an end to both of them," Gadreel said.

Crossing the River of Sin, we now stood in a weird wooded area, and towering above the trees stood what Jophiel called the Tower of Babel. "Damn, will we have to pass through that?" I asked. "I hope not, but the chances are high that you will see the inside of that hellish place," Jophiel answered. "What do you have to do wrong to end up in there?" I questioned. "Nothing, the lower demons live there. If you are unlucky enough to end up there, you will be stuck for all time," Jophiel answered. "Got it! I am not going in that damn place if I can still help it," I said, looking up to the top, which I couldn't see because it rose into the very clouds. "First, we will go to the Lake of Fire," Jophiel said, pointing back to the tower that we could see clearly from the woods. "I have a feeling King Nimrod will be around, so we will have to be quick about this once we get there," Jophiel said. I looked over at him and notice that he was walking a little fast than he was before. He wants to make it there before this Nimrod guy comes, but he was more worried about that guy in the desert somewhere in the back of my mind. The woods were thick, but I could see a red light coming from somewhere deep into the woods, to call it a forest would be a bit of an understatement. Jophiel keeps moving, and the woods started to thin out slowly before finally opening up. Well, I'll tell you one thing, when they say Lake of Fire, they weren't kidding. I was amazed at what I was looking at. It was a lake, but almost like an oil fire out at sea, the fire was at the top, and as I got closer to the lake edge, I glanced in to see a kind of lava black color. I glanced over to Jophiel, and almost like he read my mind. He pointed out to the lake. "Lake of Fire," he said. "Thanks, Jophiel. I wouldn't have figured it out without you" I smiled.

Lake of Fire & Tukuk

Jophiel went to one knee, took out the holy cloth, and walked over to me. "Come, Freddie, I must ready you for your test," Jophiel said. I looked over to him and then back to the lake's edge. "Okay, where is Tukuk?" I asked. Jophiel started to wrap the parts of my skin that weren't cover in holy cloth. "Tukuk is at the center of the lake. You must swim to him and touch him. Once you do that, it will be all up to you, Freddie," Jophiel answered. "No pressure," I said. "Freddie, you must think of this as an all or nothing. If you can't make it to Tukuk's body, the flames will burn you to your very soul. And there's something else though," Jophiel said. I looked over at him. "Well, let's hear it then," I snapped. "If Tukuk finds your soul unfit to use his power, he will destroy it as well," Jophiel said. "You said he was dead," I said. "Yes, in body, but his soul is still very much alive," Jophiel murmured. Great, I was at the edge of the lake, and my human side was having second thoughts about this whole thing. "Just wish me luck," I said, taking in a deep breath. "Luck will have nothing to do with it. Think faith, my friend," Jophiel said. I looked into the lake and again took a deep breath, and walked into it. At this point, I thought I would burst into flames, but the holy cloth held firm as I pulled my head under the fire.

The first thing I noticed once I got in was that I was glowing. I looked to my arm, and it was the holy cloth that was shining. I started swimming and couldn't see about ten feet in front of me. *Better hurry*, I said to myself. I could feel my body starting to burn a little bit at my feet, but I kept swimming. The deeper I went, the hotter it got, and the more worried I got. *Where is this fucker at?* I snapped to myself. Then from the corner of my eye, I saw a large box sitting at the bottom of the lake. Well, good news, I found it. I need air. My lungs by this time burned for air, but I didn't have time to go back up to get air and try to find it again. Then I remembered what Jophiel said, *think faith*, I thought to myself and kept swimming until I touched the box which I discovered was a casket. I tried to pull it open, but the damn thing wouldn't move. My lungs were already screaming at me for air, and I tried one more time, and it opened. I stuck my hand inside and touch the first thing I could, and that was when a thing opened up.

I opened my eyes, and I was in darkness. I couldn't see a damn thing, and that's when a voice spoke. "Who are you, human?" the voice asked. At first, I didn't know where the voice was coming from, but then I figured out, it was coming from all around me. At once, I answered. "Freddie Johnson. Who are you, sir?" I said, trying to sound as strong as I could. The voice answered back with a laugh. "I think you already know who I am." My human side was scared in the worst way. "I'm here to use your power. I'm trying to go back home," I shouted. "Well, I figured that. A human here in hell is a bad time for anyone," the voice said. "You are Tukuk, right?" I questioned. "Yes, human. I am he. The one whose skin made it impossible for even the Creator to get rid of me," Tukuk said. "Yeah, that what I've heard from a friend," I said. "Oh, do I know this friend of yours, human?" Tukuk asked. "I don't think so. Not unless you know angels," I answered. "I only knew two in my whole time up there. Michael and Jophiel," Tukuk said. I looked around for something, anything that would tell me where I was. "You wish to see me in person?" Tukuk asked. "No, not if you don't want to," I answered quickly. I didn't want to piss off a demon like this, and I wanted to keep him as happy as possible. Just then, a flame appeared about seven feet away from me and rose high into the air, if I could call it the sky. Something appeared in the fire, small at first, but it soon grew about nine feet with coal-like eyes. "Here I am, human," Tukuk said, stepping out of the flame and walking over to me. He was a giant demon, not as big as Buer but was still a mountain of monsters that I didn't want to cross. "So, which angel walks with you, boy?" Tukuk asked. "Jophiel," I answered. "Oh, I have good dealing with him," Tukuk said. His body was like the color of brick, and his face was like a stone. I couldn't tell if it helps me knowing Jophiel was a good thing or not. "If you wish to use my powers, you must do something for me, and remember, I will know if you don't," Tukuk said. "Okay, what do I have to do?" I asked. "You must return my children to power. If you do that, you will have full control of my powers at your will," Tukuk answered. I looked up at him. I think there wasn't much I could do to say no to the guy. "Okay, you got a deal," I said. The first thing I saw once those words left my mouth was that his eyes got huge, about as big as beach balls. He held out his hand. "Take my hand, human, and with it…my power," Tukuk said. I reached for his hand. The flame started to burn what was left of the holy cloth and my shirt and jeans. The flame burned me right down to my very soul, and that shit hurt.

After a few minutes, a black sphere appeared in the center of the lake. *I hope that he talked well with him as he did with Buer*, Jophiel thought. The sphere grew in size and started to spin slowly but then picked up speed as it rose into the air above the Lake of Fire. The fire followed, and the sphere soon took on the Lake of Fire, pulling the liquid from the lake and taking it into the sphere. "Well, that human must have done something right," Jophiel said. The sphere was now nothing more than fire as the lake below slowly disappeared. By the time the sphere came back down, the Lake of Fire was no more, and it hit the ground with a loud sound that sent fire into the air. Out from the top came a fire that burned the sphere away, leaving only a pair of orange eyes looking back at Jophiel. *Freddie sure knows how to make an entrance*, he thought, looking out into the flamed out lake bottom.

I first felt a warm breeze hit my ass, then realized I was naked and quickly tried to cover up. "Well, looks like you made it, and you have the power," Jophiel said. "Yes, I wish now that I had some pants too," I said, trying my best to keep my manhood from poking out and saying hi. "Here, put this on," Jophiel said, giving me the cloak. "Better than nothing," I murmured. "I will tell Uriel to bring you something to wear," Jophiel said. "Wait, you're not going with me the rest of the way?" I asked. "I wish I could, but the longer I stay, the weaker I get, and if I stayed any longer, I would die or worst….," Jophiel said. "I see, and Uriel is like you…I guess?" I questioned. "If you mean if she understands your human speak, then yes, but also like me, she doesn't know everything about your humankind," Jophiel answered. "Well, this should be fun," I said. I did feel any different than I did ten minutes ago until I stepped back on the lake edge and I saw a chunk of brimstone and touched it with my bare hand. "Well, this is great. No burn," I said like a five-year-old kid. "See, you have already found some good in it," Jophiel said. "We better get out of here. Someone might have seen that little light show," I said. Jophiel said nothing and walked off quickly with me in tow, holding a cloak around me like a middle-eastern man dress. Jophiel never took his watchfully glaze off the sky only to step over a large piece of brimstone.

Tower of Babel

Jophiel and I were waiting in the woods for something that Jophiel wouldn't say. "There's my sister," Jophiel said, looking in front of us. Out from behind a tree came Uriel. She was dressed just like Jophiel but had two bags with her. "I see you brought it," Jophiel said. "Yes, I heard that he felt funny walking around naked," Uriel said, giving me the bag. I looked inside, and my heart almost jumped out of my chest. "Pants! Oh, how I love you!" I said with too much joy in my voice. "These human things will do you better than the last pair you had," Uriel said. I started to change as Jophiel talked to Uriel about something. After they spoke for about fifteen minutes, I was changed by then and ready to take on the day. I walk over to them just as they got done talking. "I can see that you're ready," Uriel said, looking over to me. "Yes, now that I'm not naked anymore," I said. "Good luck to the both of you, and I hope to see you again, friend," Jophiel said as a light came over him, and he soon disappeared. I will tell you this much. Uriel was at least something to look at. She was about five feet six inches and had red hair with blue eyes. She seemed like a woman you could only dream for, and you would be lucky to find in your whole life. "So, where to?" I asked. "Well, we're going to try and go around the Tower of Babel and get into Sheol soon after," Uriel answered. Pointing to the mountain range behind the tower that seems to be like the Great Wall of China. "Should be easy enough," I said, walking alongside Uriel. I had a question that now filled my mind for some time, so I asked Uriel. "Uriel, are there boy and girl angels in heaven?" I asked. I know it was a stupid question to ask an angel, but I wanted to know. "If you are asking if there is a male and female sex in heaven, no, but we can take those shapes when we have to," Uriel answered, looking over at me. I could tell that she didn't know how to take that question, so I stayed quiet until Uriel spoke. "I find you odd, Freddie Johnson. You don't seem like every other human I heard about," Uriel said. I found that weird. "What do you mean by that?" I questioned. "I heard that all humans are small silly things, so far, from what I have seen from you, and what Jophiel said. You seemed different," Uriel said. I stayed silent for a minute or two until she looked over to me with those blue eyes, and I fell over a rock that was as big as a small dog. I tried my best to play it off, but I could tell she wasn't buying it. "Damn, who put that there?" my excuse with a small smile. She gave me a hand, and I took it to get me back on my feet. "I hope I don't make you feel weird," Uriel said. I looked over at her and could feel the redness came to my face. "What do you mean by that?" I asked with a cough. Uriel gave a smile, "I mean love...sex, I could say. I know nothing about that human feeling, you know?" Uriel said. I almost fell again, looking over to her. "Well, I'm not going to lie to you. You are stunning," I said. *Really, Freddie?* I told myself. If I could've slapped myself, I would have. Here I was with a hot angel woman, and I said some shit like pretty. If there were other men around, my man card would have been taking for that bullshit. Uriel stopped suddenly, and so I did. "Something is coming," Uriel whispered. "Great. Do you know a good place to hide?" I asked. "It must be King Nimrod's demons," Uriel said. Great, the second meeting I'll have with a demon in hell and me without my Sunday's best. Four tall monsters dropped from the trees that looked like they could go one round or two with Tyson.

    I stayed close, not moving an inch as the four demons moved slowly over to us. "What do you want here?" Uriel asked. The demons couldn't talk any human language, just growls and animal sounds left their mouths. I moved slowly to the left, and two of the monsters moved closer to us. They were a part of Nimrod's demon army that he made after the princes of hell were locked away by the fallen angels. "What the fuck do they want?" I asked while standing behind Uriel. I stayed back a step behind Uriel. I must have learned well from Jophiel in our time in the desert. One demon stepped forward. "You...will...come...with...us...angel scum," it stuttered. I kept my distance from Uriel. "We just wish to go to the mountains'" Uriel said. I looked over to Uriel and then back to the demons. "You could take them, right?" I asked. She said nothing at first. If there were two of them, this would be easy, but if even one got back to King Nimrod, we would be hunted down like animals. "No, we may have to play along with this until we can come up with something," she said. My look can tell Uriel a great deal...like most humans, I didn't like the fact that we had to play along. The demon that spoke pointed to the tower, "Looks like we will have to go there anyway," I murmured. We walked to the Tower of Babel with four demons keeping watch as the tower came into view.

Uriel seemed like she didn't like the idea of us going to the tower, which to me was just another tower. I could feel something in my gut that something was off. "Who is this Nimrod guy?" I whispered. Uriel didn't look back, she only spoke, "King of the Tower of Babel and the one that rules here," Uriel whispered back. I felt like a lamb being led to the cutting room floor and not getting a last meal. We reached the forest and see a large group of about fifteen of these long-neck demons. Their skin was grey with long necks, arms, and legs. They looked like a Stretch Armstrong toy that a kid stretched one time too many. Their faces were nothing but just a nose, and solid black eyes, and a smile that went from ear to ear with two rows of sharp teeth inside as one of them opened his large mouth. "Looks like they could eat a watermelon whole," I whispered. Uriel said nothing to that and looked up to the towers' top that now I couldn't see. "Listen, if King Nimrod gives you safe passage, you must take it," Uriel whispered back to me. "What? I can't leave you here," I almost shouted, but I manage to catch myself about halfway. Some of the demons looked over to me and started to sniff the air.

If they will find out that I'm a human, they will definitely try to eat me. Hopefully, we make it to Nimrod. Otherwise, they could eat us both. As we came to the gate, I could hear the screams of the human souls that now live inside. The large gate started to open slowly, the cracking sound followed. They pushed us inside, and before the gate was fully opened, we were already in the Tower of Babel.

The first thing that hit me was the smell. It was like walking into a bathroom after you take a shower. It was hot…something like water was dripping from everywhere and anywhere. "Uriel, what is this water?" I asked. "You're wrong. When they destroy a soul, that is what's left of them. Their hope and love. That's what it is," Uriel answered. I said nothing as we walked down a street where the demons would chase souls, and once they got them, it was terrible. First, they would grab the soul's head and pop it like a zit, then once the soul stopped moving, they would pull the soul apart from both arms and legs until only the center part of the soul was left. "Jesus…." I whispered. The screams echoed off the walls and the dirt streets as we walked up a set of stairs. At the top of the stairs was a man who was about two inches taller than me and was dressed in silver armor. The demon that spoke came up beside the man and pointed to us. Two monsters pushed us forward. "An angel. Well, now this is a surprise," the man said, walking over to us. "Who are you, my boy?" the man asked. "Freddie," I answered. The man now had a puzzled look on his face, "Never heard of you in the demon circles. Oh well, please, come inside," the man said. The man walked over to the large door, and two demons opened it, and we were pushed in. "I guess demons can't use words," I murmured. We have pushed along until we came to a large room with a throne made of gold in the middle of it. The man sat on the throne, and he looked over to us with a smile. "Well, I'm guessing you need to get over the mountains," the man said. "Yes, we're on a journey to the Great Power," Uriel said. I looked over at her with a bit of a smile; I guess lying to this guy is for the best. If he finds out I'm human, I wouldn't make it five minutes outside. "Well, I can't let you just past through angel. I will need something from you," the man said. "Nimrod, what is it you want?" Uriel asked as Nimrod pointed at her chest. I glanced over to them as Nimrod spoke. "I want you. Your friend can now go free, but you will stay. I will enjoy having you around, angel," Nimrod said, looking over at me. I didn't see the right hook that Nimrod threw. It hit me in the side of the face and sent me into the wall, which, thanks to Tukuk's power it might have saved my life. I sat up and looked over at Nimrod, who now was holding Uriel's hand. "Nimrod…." Uriel said. I got up and looked over at him. "You will leave Freddie, this is his own journey," Nimrod smiled. I dusted myself off and gave a small smile which Nimrod saw. Two demons grabbed me by my arms and pushed me out of the room and all the way back outside.

Thanks to Tukuk's power, I will be protected against anything that will come my way. "Don't worry, angel, he will not be harmed. As long as he doesn't come back here," Nimrod told Uriel. "I never had an angel share my bed, so this will be new for the both of us," Nimrod added. Sharing Uriel's self with a demon. "You might as well kill me now, Nimrod. I will not lay with you willingly," she said. "I know, that's why I'm going to make you the light way. Then whatever is left of you will be fed to the demons," Nimrod said with a smile. She could look at him as he pulled her along. "I could have my demons kill that Freddie thing and have them bring back his head," Nimrod said. She said nothing to this and followed him "See? How hard is that?" Nimrod mocked.

I was pushed to the main gate, and from there, they pointed to the mountain that wasn't too far away. Great, Uriel is stuck with that asshole, and I can't help her. *Jophiel, I really could use some help*, I said to myself. I started walking, feeling like I got my ass kicked by my older brother with my head down, looking at the red ground. "Keep your heart, Freddie," a voice said. I looked around then up to the sky before looking around again. "It's me, Jophiel. I'm talking with you in your mind," he said. "Good, I could use some help…I mean, Uriel could use some help. She stuck in there with demons," I said. "Keep walking friend, Gabriel will have something for you. I had hope for you not to use a weapon, but if you're going to do what I think you must do, then you will need a weapon," Jophiel said. "Sounds good. How far is Gabriel?" I asked. "Not far, I have told him about this, and he will give you two things you will be able to use," Jophiel answered. "Thanks," I said. "Don't thank me yet, Freddie," Jophiel said.

Gadreel visited someone who he thought he can help him find me. He stood in front of the door for a moment before he opened it. He stepped in only to get hit in the face and was tossed to the ground. "What is it you want here, fool?!" it asked. "Easy Azazel, I came here to talk with you," Gadreel said. Azazel stood up, and Gadreel followed. "Good to see you too," Gadreel said. "Speak fast, fool, 'cause your presence here angers me," Azazel snapped. Gadreel looked over at him. "There is an angel in hell," Gadreel said. "So what? There are fallen everywhere,"

Azazel said. "No, not this angel. He came from heaven. From the Creator's home," Gadreel said. "What does an angel from the Creator's world doing here?" Azazel asked. "I don't know, but I will tell you this. There's a human here in hell too, and the angel is helping him," Gadreel answered. "A human? You're lying!" Azazel shouted. Gadreel put up a hand and put something on the table. "Smell that then tell me that I'm lying," Gadreel said. Azazel picked up the melted black thing, smelled it, and dropped it in shock. "I see? A human shoe," Gadreel said. "This human must be brought to you so you can find out why he is here," Gadreel added. "Maybe the Creator sent him here," Azazel said. "Are you the angel of death or some…pussy?" Gadreel said. Azazel laughed at this and walked over to his window. "I care not for your human term…I want to know what this living human is doing here and then…." Azazel said. "….kill him," Gadreel finished. "Yes, kill the human and I'll place his soul in the Tower of Babel myself," Azazel said. "Sounds good to me," Gadreel said. "You and your bastard child will stay out of this until the human has been dealt with," Azazel said looking over at Gadreel. Gadreel put his hands up and walked to the door then a smile slowly came across his face.

I walked until I got to the bottom of the extensive mountain range and a trail that went to the top. There at the bottom of the course was Gabriel. "I'm glad that you're here. Uriel is in trouble," I said. "I know, Freddie. Jophiel told me everything and the fact that you want to go back in there, which is a bad idea," Gabriel said. "Well, I'm going back there with or without your help," I said. Gabriel smiled, and from his hip, he pulled out a sword. "I'm giving you my sword, and, human, use it well. It will kill any of the demons inside the tower, just don't get yourself killed," Gabriel said. I took the sword and nodded before I turned around and started to walk. "Freddie, good luck to you," Gabriel said. I smiled and ran off back to the tower.

Nimrod stood next to Uriel as he touched her arm slowly; Uriel could feel her light dim as the demon kissed her hand. "The only thing you will get out of me is my light, so you might as well take it and be done with it," Uriel said. "Uriel, my lady, I will take your light in time, but we should have some fun first," Nimrod said. He bit into her skin with his demon fangs and the pain of Uriel's light being taking away.

Uriel fell on the floor holding her arm. "Now, my dear Uriel…I will slowly suck your light away until there is nothing left of you, then I will toss you to the demons," Nimrod said with a smile.

I came up to the wall and saw a small tunnel that ran through the border into the inside. "Well, for once, I wished I played more Metal Gear Solid when I was younger," I said to myself. I crawled through the tunnel and came to a metal gate. In the end, I tried to pull it, and I was suddenly hit in the face by the small entrance. "Hero foul…" I said, rubbing my face. Before I could come out, the sounds of feet made me stop, and I saw a soul hit the ground about ten feet away. I watched as the demons ripped it apart. Cries fill the tunnel, and I had to turn away from it. Once the screams had stopped, the only thing left was a puddle of what I could only say was water. The demons stood there for a moment before they ran off chasing down another soul. "Jophiel," I whispered. "Yes, Freddie, what is it?" Jophiel asked. "I thought there weren't souls in Limbo?" I asked, moving behind a wall across from the tunnel. "Yes, I told you, right? They must be getting them from the Aokigahara," Jophiel answered. I looked up at the stairs where the demons pushed me down earlier. "What will happen to Uriel?" I asked. "He will take her light and have the demon eat her body," Jophiel answered. I stopped and almost fell down after hearing it. "You think you can lead me to her?" I questioned. "Yes, but you will have to go to the top of the tower. You might not be able to get out the way you came in," Jophiel answered. Great, how in the hell I'm I going to get to the top of this motherfucking building? I can't even see the top of it. I pulled out Gabriel's sword and looked over to the door where two demons were doing their watch, but they were sitting on the ground. One was sleeping, and the other was chewing on a soul's arm. I pulled the cloak's hood over my head and walked up to the door. The demon that was chewing on the arm looked at me and didn't move from his arm. I couldn't believe how close I was to this demon. I could spit on him any time. I had Gabriel's sword ready, and in one motion I cut the top of the demon's head off. He screamed out, and I quickly gutted him and his friend open. The sleeping demon didn't see it coming. I quickly ran inside and shut the door, making sure that I was clear. Now I stood in a large hallway, and I moved over to a statue sitting to my left. "You must go to the end of the hallway and make a right," Jophiel said. I waited to make sure there weren't any more demons coming; and ran down to the end of the hallway and looked down the right side, and I saw Nimrod. "I hate that fuck face," I said under my breath. I looked back down the hallway and saw Nimrod and two other demons holding Uriel. She looked like an African child you might see on one of those "feed the children." Her bones were showing, and she looked different already. "Jophiel, she looks bad. Is there a way to help her?" I asked. "I will tell you once you get hold of her, but right now, you must hurry," Jophiel answered. That's right, I killed those demons at the front door. It won't be long until someone comes along. I followed Nimrod and his boy, hiding when I need to and keeping myself in the shadows, which were many in a place like this. They put her in a room two floors up, and one of the demons was left there outside the door. I could hear a bit of what Nimrod was saying. "Good. Now, find that Freddie thing and kill him." Great, so much for keeping his word, lying piece of shit. I waited until they walked away, and just then, a sound filled the tower. "Fuck! That must be the alarm," I murmured. I ran down the hallway at full speed, right at the demon that was too busy looking around to see me coming.

    I could feel the power all throughout my body. *Creator...help me*, I called. Suddenly, a sound filled the room, like demonic yelling that could cause me great pain if I was any weaker. The door opened, and a human appeared holding a sword that could have belonged to only one I knew. "What...are...you doing?" I asked. The human looked over to me and helped me up. "I'm getting you out of here, now!" he said, lifting me off the stone-ground into his chest. "You shouldn't be here, it's not safe," I said, unable to talk right anymore. This human is indeed a strange one. Never in my life have I ever met one like him.

    I was carrying Uriel into the hallway and hoped the top wasn't that far. "Jophiel, I have Uriel," I said. I looked over to her and saw nothing but skin and bones. Her blue eyes were primarily white, and her once long red hair turned white, and she looked like an old woman, no longer the pretty angel I came herewith. I moved quickly to the stairs and started going up, moving as soon as possible with an angel that now weighed sixty pounds. "Hurry, Freddie, I can sense them coming," Jophiel said.

Nimrod was walking to the front of his throne when two demons came in and others in tow behind him. Four were carrying two demon bodies with them. "Who did this?" Nimrod asked. The demons looked at each other, and all of them shook their heads. "You mean to tell me that none of you know who did this…useless bastard!" Nimrod shouted and kicked one in the chest, sending him to the ground. "Find who did this, or I will slaughter every single one of you. Go!" Nimrod yelled, pointing to the door. The demons ran around like chickens with their heads cut off. "That thing called Freddie, I should have had him killed when I had the chance," Nimrod whispered under his breath.

After what felt like forever, finally, I saw the top of the stairs and the red sky. "Jophiel, I'm at the top. How in the hell are we going to get out of here?" I asked. "Uriel will have to take part of your soul. She will regain her power and will be able to get you out of there," Jophiel answered. "Okay, Uriel, you're going to have to take part of my soul for us to get out of here," I said. Uriel was having trouble breathing, and I could tell that whatever that sound was, it's making her worst. "But… you…might die," she stuttered. "Well, there's always a first time for everything," I smiled, helping her to stand. I could hear the sounds of footsteps coming up the stairs. "Get ready," Uriel said, putting her boney hand on my chest. Suddenly I felt cold like, I stepped outside in subzero weather and a blind light filled the sky. I fell to one knee as Uriel rose high in the sky wrapped with a warm light. "Freddie, take my hand!" she shouted. I reached up and grabbed her hand and, with superhuman strength, lifted me up into the air with one arm, and I looked at her face. She was young again, and her red hair looked like it was on fire, and her blue eyes looked at me as she took off through the air.

This human must have been helped by Jophiel to get inside. And now he was looking at me with a look of love and shock in those eyes of his, Uriel thought. "Hang on, Freddie. I'm going to take you to Gabriel. He should be able to help you," she whispered. I smiled at her weakly as she flew through the air. Uriel saw Gabriel at the mountain pass and flew over to his land softly with me in her hand. "This belongs to you," I said, giving him back his sword. "Good, now that you two are here, I can have this place destroyed," Gabriel said. Uriel held me close as one of her most powerful brothers came to destroy the tower.

First, I thought I was dreaming until I looked up in the sky and saw a light. "What's that?" I asked. Uriel, who still had a hold of me, looked up to the sky. "It's our big brother. An angel of the highest class," Uriel explained. From light, a shape came into view like a wagon wheel but bigger. As the size of the moon is the only thing I could think of, it was cover in the eyes of every color. "That's a real big brother," I said. "It's a throne, known to us as the Great Wheel," Gabriel said. The throne float was floating, and a powerful bolt of light came from the center. I'm not talking about the lightning you see during a thunderstorm. I'm talking millions of times more powerful and that if I'm right. The lightning hit the Tower of Babel, and it was like watching a flash of lightning hit a tree. The bolt went straight to the ground, and a booming sound followed, and the tower leaned right until it fell over, crashing to the ground and destroying anything left of it. A large cloud of dust and dirt went into the air. "We better go before they try to come after us," Gabriel said. I tried to walk, but that just wasn't happening, and Uriel had to help me. "You better let me help you until your soul gets stronger again," Uriel said. I looked into her blue eyes and was thinking the whole time that I just save an angel. Cool, right?

Year 2: Ziz & the Power

We walked into the mountains until Gabriel thought it was safe, and the three of us stopped. I still felt exhausted from letting Uriel take some of my soul to get out of the Tower of Babel, but we were both alive, so that's good. "Are you okay, Freddie?" Gabriel asked, stopping in front of us. "I'll be fine once we get somewhere safe," I answered, trying to sound durable, but if anything, by the sound of my voice, I was weak. "We will stop up there. No one from Babel would come after us right now if any of them left," Gabriel said. Gabriel sounded like a marine. The next thing I was waiting for him to say was, let's go back and double tap some fools, but that would be too much. Uriel was still with us and looking a lot better than she did at the tower. She had her glow back and seemed more worried about me than I was about her. "We will be stopping soon, so just hang on," Uriel said. Most of the walk I could manage, but now I felt sleepy and saw Uriel and Gabriel doubled. "Jesus...." I said, stopping suddenly and leaning against Uriel, who came up to help me walk. Gabriel pointed to a bend up ahead, and I manage to get to that without much trouble. After Uriel sat me down, I passed out right there on the ground.

I was lying on the ground, and Gabriel went over to me. "He's fine, Uriel, but, his soul is weak. He needs the light," Gabriel said. "I can't give him much. I used most of the power on getting us out," Uriel said. "Then both of us have to use our light together and hope he wakes soon," Gabriel said as his wings appeared. He put his hands together, and light slowly appeared in front of his face. "Here, you will have to give it to him," Gabriel said. His wings turning into the sand as Uriel took hold of Gabriel's light. "Once you do that, you better get out of here, otherwise, we might have more demons coming," Gabriel said. "Okay," she said. Uriel took in Gabriel's light, and her wings soon appeared, and she took hold of me holding me tight. "I have a feeling that Freddie will wake a pleased human," Gabriel murmured.

    I woke to the smell of flowers, and I looked up to Uriel holding tight to her body and a warming light around her. "Uriel...?" I said, looking her in the face. Her blue eyes looked down at me, and she smiled. "Sorry, I had to use the light to heal your soul. You should be fine now," Uriel said. *Wait a minute, I'm in the arms of a hot angel chick? I think I now know what heaven feels like*, I thought. "Uriel, you just made me the happiest human ever," I said. "See Uriel, I told you, a happy human," Gabriel said with a smile. I looked over to Gabriel, who had a big smile at Uriel. I only hope that she didn't get it. "What do you mean by that?" Uriel asked. Gabriel put his hand up and said nothing. "Wait, how did Nimrod take your light?" I asked. "He bit me into my skin and took it out through his teeth," Uriel answered. "Oh, so like a vampire," I said. "What is this...vampire?" Uriel asked. "Something we humans made up that sucks blood from humans to stay alive," I answered. "Well, in that case, yes, Nimrod would be a vampire," Uriel said. "Thank goodness we got rid of that guy," I murmured. "Don't be so sure, Freddie. Nimrod is a demon...he might have survived," Gabriel said. "What, are you kidding me? That bastard got blown up by a Throne! He couldn't have survived that!" I said. The shock on my face couldn't be more black and white. "Nimrod was wearing the Armor of Satan. He could've survived it," Gabriel said. I couldn't believe what I was hearing. It was like if you drop a five thousand pound bomb on a bunch of Taliban guys and find out that they lived and had tea in the rubble. "And hopefully he will stay away from us?" I questioned. Gabriel said nothing, and he had no expression on his face, and it was like playing poker with a card shark. "Has anyone told you, Gabriel, that you have a good poker face?" I said. "No, what is a poker?" Gabriel asked. "A card game, you know? Like gin and spades?" I said. This must be a first because Gabriel made a puzzled look as I sat up. "I will take that as a no," I added. "I know about humans.

Not about card games," Gabriel said. "You said the Armor of Satan as in the Satan?" I asked. Gabriel looked over at me. "Yes, it was for the horseman war. The one that will take peace from the earth when the time comes," Gabriel answered. "Wow, wait, so the world will end soon?" I questioned. "I can't tell you that, but you should be ready, Freddie," Gabriel answered. I looked up at the red sky and wonder what was happening back on earth. Did anyone remember me coming? I'm still out on the road sitting in a destroyed car. I couldn't think about that stuff. Now just have to get through this and will figure the rest out. I slowly fell asleep in Uriel's arms again wonder what was going on down on earth.

Gabriel looked over to us, and Uriel saw that he pointed at me. Uriel checked to see if I was really asleep, which I was. "What's going on, Gabriel?" she asked. "Michael was talking with me about him, and from what I heard, I couldn't believe it myself," Gabriel answered. "What do you mean? If it wasn't for him, I would still be in the tower," Uriel said. Gabriel held up his hand, and Uriel stopped talking. "I know, but the boy is something that Michael has been looking for since the Great Flood," Gabriel said. "What is he then?" Uriel asked. "I don't know. Michael didn't tell me much. So, I can only go off of what I heard from Jophiel, who never hides anything from anyone," Gabriel said. "You mean...." Uriel started to say it until it pops into her head, and even then, she couldn't believe it. "The *Redeemer*, the first since the Great Flood," Gabriel said. "But there hasn't been a *Redeemer* since Peter. How do you know this?" Uriel asked. "As I said, I only know what Jophiel told me. At first, Michael wanted to start the journey with him, but Jophiel said it was too soon to tell him. Which was wise, base off two close calls he has so far," Gabriel said. "I hope you're wrong," Uriel murmured. "I hope so too, but so far, the human hasn't failed yet, and if this keeps going, I might have to change my tune," Gabriel said. Uriel looked down at me, while I was sleeping peacefully in her arms. "I know what you're thinking, Uriel, but you can't be with him. One, he's a human, two, he has a job to do, but that might change the world," Gabriel said. "Then you know what might happen to you if this is true," Uriel said. "Yes, I know. I will die" Gabriel murmured. Uriel hated the way he said that almost as if he welcomed it. "Sometimes, Gabriel, you scare me, and I'm your sister. What if Freddie saves you, what then?" Uriel asked. "Then I guess I will be eating my words, then," Gabriel answered with a smile. Uriel looked down at me, while I was still sleeping, and she wondered if I could do it.

I woke to Uriel standing up, her light was gone. Gabriel stood next to me and held out his hand. "We need to leave this place. I'm not sure if Nimrod is still alive," Gabriel said. "Okay," I said, standing up. "I wish the two of you the best of luck," Uriel said as her light blinded me, and she was gone seconds later. "So, where to now?" I asked. "We will go as far as we can into the mountains, then we will have to catch a ride on Ziz," Gabriel answered. I looked over at him, "Who's Ziz?" I asked. "The Great Sky Monster that lives here once we go about halfway, the only way to get through will be with Ziz," Gabriel answered. We started to walk, and I felt the wind picked up, and it started to get colder. "Good thing I have the cloak. Otherwise, I would be freezing right now," I said. I could see that we would reach the top of this mountain and might be able to look at onto the mountains to see everything. The closer to the top we got, the harder it was to breathe. "Gabriel, how high are these mountains?" I asked. "They reach to the roof of hell in some places, but this is as high as we should get until we ride on Ziz," Gabriel answered, looking back at me. Felt like I was breathing through a straw, but I tried to walk on, trying to get as much distance from the tower as we could.

Gadreel flew over what was left of the Tower of Babel, which wasn't much, as he spotted a group of demons pulling something from the rubble. "You demon, where is Nimrod?" Gadreel asked. The monster said nothing. Instead, it only pointed to someone standing on top of what was left of the wall that protected the tower. Gadreel floated over to the person and saw that it was Nimrod. "What happened here, friend?" Gadreel asked. "Fucking angels…." Nimrod said, tossing a piece of stone to the ground. "I'm sorry for your loss, but I'm looking for a said angel. They have a human with them, and I'm guessing you had a run-in with them too," Gadreel murmured. "If you're asking where they are, I have no idea. If I knew I would be sending my demons after them to kill them and bring back their dead bodies," Nimrod said. "We might be able to help each other, friend. You need demons. Nephilims that can catch them. I need someone that can lead them, we can help each other kill our enemies," Gadreel said. "I wish to take them myself. Why should I join forces with you fallen? You are the last one I would want to work with," Nimrod said. "It's because your demons can see them from miles away, but my children, they can't see them coming. Everyone gets what they want, you get the human that I know is with them, and I get the angel," Gadreel murmured. Nimrod looked over at Gadreel and nodded at him as they shook hands. "So, what's your plan, fallen?" Nimrod asked. "First, we need to know where they're heading to and I think I know where," Gadreel answered, pointing to the mountains. "Impossible, they would need Ziz to help them, and he's sleeping. They would have to get the *Power* to wake him up, and many demons have tried to get it even the Lord of the Flies couldn't get it," Nimrod said. "Would you like to bet that they know of a way to wake him up?" Gadreel said. "I will leave for the Power as soon as your Nephilims are ready," Nimrod said. "Good, and thank you again for your help," Gadreel said.

Gabriel didn't tell me that it would get this cold. I could feel it through my skin that was made new by Tukuk. I have a feeling that I would have been frozen by now. "From here, you can see most of the mountains," Gabriel said, pointing across to a beam of light that was out in the distance. "What's that?" I asked, pointing to the light. "That's the Great Power. The Lord of the Flies took it from your world long ago and keeping it here for himself," Gabriel answered. "You mean it was something important?" I questioned. "Yes, the Princes of Hell took anything and everything they could from you," Gabriel answered. I saw that the trail took us across the vast gap between this mountain range and the next one. "Sounds like a riot," I said. "A riot. What is that?" Gabriel asked. "Something humans do while they tear up someone else's stuff and stealing. There's a shit ton of that going on, too," I answered. Gabriel gave a puzzled look. "Hopefully, this thing will hold us," I murmured. "We'll find out," Gabriel said, stepping on the bridge. Yeah, he could be a marine in my world for sure. I followed his lead, but I made sure that the bridge would take me at every step. Just because I have Tukuk's power, I don't really want to use it or test it like this. About half way, Gabriel looked up, and my gaze followed him till I saw that the red sky became dark, and something blocked the light. "Gabriel...what is... that?" I asked, not taking my eyes off the thing in the sky. "That...my friend, Freddie, is the Sky Monster, Ziz, the one that will block out the

Creator's sun," Gabriel answered. I couldn't tell if Gabriel was scared or amazed at this monster. From what I could see, he was big. His wings were blocking the light, and I could only make out the wings that looked like something from a Bald Eagle. I had walked right up on Gabriel, watching this animal or monster flap its wings. A gust of wind followed. "I think I know where the wind is coming from!" I shouted to Gabriel. Gabriel was holding on to the bridge as Ziz's wings returned to where ever they came from. "We must go to him and hope he will take us the rest of the way!" Gabriel shouted. The wind was still blowing even after Ziz stops flapping his wings. "No one told me that a thing like this was down here!" I shouted. "You didn't see the Watchers, Freddie?!" Gabriel shouted back. I nodded yes, but even then, I didn't think it would get this big. "There are three of them, one of the sky, one of ground, and one of the seas!" Gabriel shouted. The wind started to die down, and I could hear myself think again. "How often does he do that?" I asked, talking normal again. "Whenever he wants to, no one can tell him to stop," Gabriel answered. We stepped onto the other side and kept an eye on the sky to see if I could see this Ziz. "So, why do we need a ride? Can't we just fly across?" I asked. "I would like to, but the Fallen would find us, and we don't need that. Plus, it's a long way to fly. It would take me a year to fly us, but with Ziz, we will be there in no time," Gabriel answered. "I see. Jophiel told me that the fallen guy could sense you, so I see the point," I said. "Well, there is more than just one of them. There is five total, and they live in parts of hell. So it best to just to try and make it without using my angelic powers," Gabriel said. "So, these Fallens are like your brothers at one point in time?" I asked. "Yes, until they cover the Creator's world with their half children call Nephilims, and the Creator was forced to flood the world," Gabriel answered. "Now I see why they might not like you," I said. "When your humankind was young, we stayed close to you, and some of us angels had a feeling for your human women. Let's just say that was something the Creator couldn't stay for," Gabriel said. I looked up to the red sky and saw something moving high, and I stopped. "Gabriel, what is that?!" I asked, pointing up to the sky. Gabriel looked up and stopped. "Damn, they couldn't know that we came this way," Gabriel whispered. I stopped and looked over at Gabriel, who didn't move at all. "I'm guessing this is not part of the plan?" I said. "It's Yeqon. Damn, that means Gadreel will not be far behind," Gabriel said. I looked up at the angel that was floating there. "So, there are more than five of these guys?" I questioned. "Yes, hundreds of them, but most are weaker than us. There are five that we have to worry about," Gabriel said, hugging the side of the mountain and slowly walking. I followed his lead and saw that the angel hadn't seen us and floated off. "So, these five fallens are the ones we're trying to avoid?" I asked. "Yes, at one point, they shared the same rank of the archangel as I and the others," Gabriel answered. Great, so these angels are just as strong as Gabriel and the others. *I see why they aren't trying to fly and do all that other crazy shit*, I thought, as Gabriel looked around the bend. "We'll have to fine Ziz quickly and get to the Great Power as soon as we can," Gabriel said. I said nothing, just nodded as we came around the bend and ran down the trail.

Azazel floated down to Gadreel and Nimrod. "Jesus, you didn't tell me you got Azazel with you too," Nimrod said with a troubled look on his face. "I know, but I didn't know that he would come here," Gadreel said with a small smile. "I see you weren't kidding about angels in hell, but I don't see a human," Azazel said. "I saw him. The human," Nimrod murmured. "So, you were telling the truth. I'm glad that I don't have to kill you now," Azazel said. "I sent Yeqon ahead to see if he could find them. I also have the others coming and will meet us in the Forest of Suicide," Gadreel said. "You think they will head through the mountains? It will take them ten years to get through there," Nimrod said. "I know, unless they get a ride on Ziz," Gadreel said, putting his hands on his face. "Ziz, you mean that damn sky beast? I cursed that monster," Azazel said. "Then we better go get them. Nimrod, take the Nephilims with you. They should be able to catch up with them," Gadreel said, looking over to Nimrod. Nimrod said nothing, only nodded as he flew off. "It will be nice to see a brother or sister. It's been so long," Gadreel said with a smile.

Gabriel watched overhead for some time now and didn't see anything yet. He knew that only one brother of him would come to face him, and that is Gadreel. That fool knowing him he will try to bring his children in force through the mountains only to find out that they will be suck and we should be gone by then. "Freddie, very soon, we'll have to take that ride. You're going to have to follow my lead," he said. I looked over at him and nodded as we came to the bottom of the trail. Jophiel did say that humans are wise when it comes to war...this didn't surprise him. Humans are constantly fighting each other, he couldn't blame us. It wasn't long ago that he went to war against his fallen brothers and sister and didn't think a second about them afterward. We came to the end of the trail and saw me in front of him. He looked back at me standing next to him with a puzzled look on my face. "We're here, Freddie," Gabriel said. He only heard me murmured a single word, *fuck*!

I had just got a four-letter word out of my mouth when I saw that we came to a mirror-like glass with our reflections looking back at us. "Gabriel...what...is...this?!" I stuttered. "Ziz, the beast of the sky," Gabriel said. His gaze turned upward, and I saw that this mirror was large, very...huge. Then I realized...."this is his fucking eye!" I shouted. Gabriel said nothing but the smile on his face answered that question. The eye closed and opened before it lifted into the air. I could see feathers as the eye and part of its head disappeared into the mist covering the mountains. "Gabriel, it's good to see you again. It has been too long since I have seen you," the voice boomed. "Ziz, my old friend, it's good to see you too. I need some help getting through the mountain. Can you help me?" Gabriel shouted. "Yes, I do owe you from the Great Flood. Get on my head, friend, and hang on," the voice boom and the eye return to us. Gabriel grabbed hold of me at my waist. "Easy with the hand, friend," I said. Gabriel jumped high into the sky until the eye was below us, and we held on to some feather on the side of what I think was his face. "We must be on the top of his head. One more jump might do it!" Gabriel shouted, throwing both of us into the air until I could see the top of Ziz's head. I could see a yellow beak, and the feathers on his head were brown with a black spot like the size of a lake on the top of his head. "Wow, this guy is huge!" I shouted, looking around at the mountains. "Ziz, we are on your head at the very top," Gabriel called. "Good, hang on," Ziz boomed, and I could feel the G-Force as Ziz went through the air and stopped in the sky. "Jesus...." I said, trying to hold on. I looked to my left and saw a large wing. I never saw anything this big before in my life. His wings stretched so far that I couldn't see its end. Ziz got into the air with one mighty flap. We were in the air just above the mountain, and with another, he was off through the sky. The wind came across Gabriel and me like we were both in a hurricane. The only thing saving us was that Gabriel used his wings to keep the wind out of our faces. "The only way to fly!" I shouted. Gabriel nodded, looking forward to Ziz at the light that we saw back on the ground. I noticed that the light was coming from a large building that looked like the White House. "That's where we're going first!" Gabriel shouted. "Ziz, we need you to take us over there to the Great Power?" Gabriel shouted. "You know who is imprisoned there, right?" Ziz boomed. "Yes, but I need what is inside there," Gabriel called. "Very well then, hang on," Ziz said, turning to the right, and we saw that the light was now ahead of us. "Gabriel, who is imprisoned there?" I shouted. "The Lord of the Flies. One of the Princes of Hell," Gabriel answered. "I'm guessing you, and he doesn't get along?" I asked. "You could say something like that," Gabriel answered. Ziz landed, sending pieces of the mountain crashing to the ground below us, and it was a long way down.

Well, making it to the Great Power was easy. Now came the hard part of taking something from a demon and one of the Princes of Hell. "Freddie, follow me and stay close," Gabriel said. I nodded as he grabbed hold of my side. "We're going to have a nice long talk about two men and holding a guy's waist," I said. Gabriel ignored me and jumped of Ziz to the ground landing softly with his wings. "Come, we must be quick about this. If Gadreel is chasing us, he will not be far behind," he said. I walked quickly behind him as we came to the front door of the large house. "This place looks like the White House," I said. "What type of house is that?" Gabriel asked. "In my world, it's a place where the most powerful person in the world stays," I answered. He said nothing to that as he opened the door and walked inside.

The place was prominent, but it was more like a fake front. Inside about twenty feet away, was a large fence that ran into the stone. "What the hell is this?!" I snapped. "The fallen made it for him," Gabriel said, pointing to the fence. I looked up to see two large eyes looking back at us, and by the looks of them, they looked like compound eyes, like something you might see on a fly. "What the...." I said. "So, Gabriel, it's good to see you again, angelic piece of shit," a voice said. From the sound of that voice, he was pissed and might have had good reason to be. "Who is that?" I whispered. "One of the Princes of Hell...Beelzebub, *Lord of the Flies,*" Gabriel said. Just when he said that a buzzing sound could be heard, like an angry lawn tool. "Well, what do we have here? A human and he has the power Tukuk, my father. You winged piece of shit you gave my father's power to some fucked monkey?!" Beelzebub snapped. "I should be offended by that," I whispered. "Yes, the human indeed has your father's power, but I didn't help him get it. He got it himself, with his own strength," Gabriel shouted. "And that means what to me, Gabriel?!" Beelzebub snapped. The buzzing sound returned but this time, louder than before. "Wait a minute, hello, Freddie Johnson, the monkey!" I murmured. His eyes looked down at me, and I looked up to where his eyes were. "Yes, I jumped into the Lake of Fire to get this power. I met your father, I guess I could say that. We need something called the Great Power, could you help us?" I asked. "You manage to live through the Lake of Fire? But you are a human. That is impossible. What do they call you?" Beelzebub asked. I looked to Gabriel, who said nothing but waved me on as I stepped in front of him. "Freddie Johnson," I said. "Could be...." Beelzebub said before breaking into a kind of laugh, kind of cried. "Well, Gabriel, you have always been the one angel that would keep odd company," Beelzebub added. I felt like they were having a secret conversation with each other, and I was left out. "Go ahead then, Freddie Johnson, but if you are who I think you are, say *hi* to your papa, boy," Beelzebub smiled. I looked at him with a puzzled looked on my face as Gabriel grabbed my shoulder. "We need to get up there," Gabriel said. He pointed to the beam of light that disappeared into the red sky. "What the hell is that?" I asked. "The Great Power," Gabriel answered.

 Gabriel had hoped that Beelzebub wouldn't tell me too much about myself until Michael got to me. Thankfully Beelzebub is a bit of a fool, and I seemed not to follow what he said, but Gabriel couldn't be too sure. I had some tact with Beelzebub and could ask me a question about my father or mother at any time, but he said nothing. I followed Gabriel into the tunnel that leads to the Great Power. "Are you sure this is the way?" I asked. "Yes, but we'll need to be quick. I don't know if Gadreel has stopped looking for us," Gabriel answered. I was still looking at Gabriel, and he could tell what that look was about, but I was walking quickly behind him in the meantime. The only light in the tunnels came from holes made in the roof of the tunnel. It would be the first time Gabriel would see the Great Power himself, and being in front of it was odd for him. "Okay, Freddie, you're going to have to take a leap of faith," Gabriel said. "What?" Freddie asked, looking down into the hole of white light. I looked over at him and took a step back before running and jumping into the white light.

"Fuck!" I shouted, hitting something hard, and looked around from what I thought was the ground. "What the hell?" I murmured. The white light was all around me, and I couldn't say anything, and the air was heavy. "Hello?!" I yelled as I looked around. It was like a white piece of paper wrapped around me. I wish that, for once, these angels would tell me what the hell is going on before I jumped into something. I felt like everyone knew about everything, except me. "I plan to ask Gabriel what the fuck is going on!" I shouted. I looked over to my right and saw a tombstone about five feet away. "That wasn't there before," I said, walking over to it. The monument was written in some kind of language that I couldn't read. "So, who are you?" I asked myself. I touched the stone, and the white world changed to sand, and I stood up quickly. "Well, that escalated quickly," I murmured. I was standing before a man on horseback. He was looking out for something behind me. I turned to see a building out in the distance. The man on the horse was tall, about six feet ten inches, and had black hair under a brown cloak. "Who is this guy?" I asked myself. The man moved the horse forward as the sand started to turn white, and once again, I was back in this plain place. The tombstone appeared again, and this time I could read it. "Gilga…mesh," I said to myself. Then I froze, "Gilgamesh…a fucking god?!" I said. I touched the stone, and this time I felt something I couldn't explain, but it was like my soul was on fire. The light started to turn brown, and I jumped back. I was amazed that first, I jumped almost twenty feet, and second, that the ground slowly opened to a bottom that was a really steep drop. I picked myself up off the ground, and I felt a hand grab my shoulder, and I looked up to see Gabriel smiling down at me. "You didn't tell me that the Great Power was a god, a man or something by the name of Gilgamesh," I said. "I didn't know that either, friend," Gabriel said. I could feel the ground under us started to give way, "We need to go!" Gabriel snapped, pulling on my arm. I ran forward, and as soon as I took two steps, I was nine steps ahead of Gabriel. We ran out of the tunnel, and to Ziz. He flapped his wings as the mountains started to rumble. The White House-like building fell in on itself as we made it to Ziz's talon. "What's going on?!" I asked. The white light that went into the sky was now gone. The rumbling seemed to grow louder as pieces of the mountains started to turn to rubble before my eyes. "Without the Great Power, the mountains are falling," Gabriel said as Ziz rose into the sky. "If you waited any longer, they would have buried you there, friend," Ziz boomed. "I like to know what you know if you don't mind!" I shouted. "I will tell you everything once we land," Gabriel called back. I rolled my eyes and looked down to the ground and saw the craziest thing I've ever seen. Coming out from what was left of the White House-like building was the world's most enormous fly-looking thing I've ever seen. "Gabriel, what is that?!" I shouted over to him. He smiled. "It's Beelzebub," Gabriel shouted back. Well…I see why they call him that. The Lord of Flies was about as big as a Greyhound bus. From his back came four pairs of wings and made a buzzing that lifted him into the air. That's when something hit Ziz, causing us to drop suddenly. "What the fuck!" I shouted.

I shouted something, but Gabriel didn't listen. From behind, he saw a blade land into Ziz's back. "Gadreel!" Gabriel cried, looking around. "Gabriel, brother, it's good to see you!" a voice shouted back. Ziz recovered quickly, and we were flying close to what was left of the mountains. "Gabriel, where are you going with that human?" the voice shouted as Ziz was hit again. This time, however, Ziz cried out as another hit shook through his body. "Gabriel, what's going on?!" I shouted. "Gadreel has found us," he screamed and started to climb. I followed as we climbed to the top. We got to his wings when something grabbed Gabriel's leg. He looked down to see a Nephilim trying to pull him off, "What the fuck?!" Gabriel heard me said something until something grabbed me and pulled me out of his sight.

I got grabbed by one of those Nephilim things. I learned from this meeting that one needs to take a shower, and two, they need some dental care. "Hey, you big ass corn fed son of a bitch!" I shouted, slapping the thing in the face. It pulled me to him and smiled his gap-tooth smile.

"Human meat," it said. "You seem to need a toothbrush and a high school education!" I shouted. He screamed something up to the sky that I did not understand, as something came down, that same thing that chased Jophiel and me in the desert. "Well, what do we have here?" the voice boomed. I looked over to see a Nephilim trying to pull Gabriel off. I elbowed the Nephilim in the face and heard a crack sound as he fell off the back of Ziz. "Well, you must have the Great Power, so you're the one that was with Jophiel," the voice said. I was trying to keep a hold of Ziz and look at this angel that was now floating about ten feet away. "I hope you don't think you will escape me," he said. This angel was nothing like Gabriel. First off, he had an evil look to him. Second, his wings were black as charcoal, and he had a long blade with him that looked like it could do some damage. "What is it you want?" I asked him. "Your death, human," he answered. I knew that was bad, and from the look of it, we were about to be done. "I could use some help here," I murmured as I looked up to the sky. The angel lifted his blade into the air and looked down at me as he started to bring it down. I closed my eyes as a loud metallic sound filled my ears, and when I opened my eyes, I saw Gabriel standing before me. His sword was blocking the blade. "Thank God," I murmured under my breath as Gabriel stood in front of me. "Brother, it's good to see you again," he said. "I don't feel the same way," Gabriel said. I could only wonder what Gabriel was thinking about this guy.

Gadreel, the one fell that he could go without seeing. Gadreel was once a great angel. His work was heard all throughout the entire kingdom, just about every of his brother and sister knew about them. When the Creator told them to love the human, he was the one that followed that rule without question. But then, one day, he left, and went to earth and even fell in love with one of them, breaking the great law. He was the reason why the Great Flood happened and why an angel can't live with a human. "Tell me, brother? Ahat are you doing with a human?" Gadreel asked. "I don't have to answer that question, brother," Gabriel answered. I was standing behind him, watching Gadreel as he landed in front of Gabriel. I could hear the sounds of Ziz's pain. He was having trouble staying in the sky, and very soon, he might drop into the ground below us. "I knew you or Michael might one day come, so I got a little from the Forest of Suicide," Gadreel said with a smile. He brought his sword down again, and a metallic clang sound echoed around us. Then I heard Ziz cry out in pain again as Gabriel knocked Gadreel back and looked over at his wing. About six Nephilims were cutting at his skin, and two of them had managed to take a chunk of his wing off. "I think this ride is done," I said. "They will take Ziz apart, and soon you will tell me anything I want to know," Gadreel said. "We got three coming behind you!" I shouted. Gabriel knew what he was talking about, and he didn't need to look back to learn. Gadreel's Nephilim children have got on Ziz while we were taking off. "You're going to have to handle them, Freddie," Gabriel said. "Sounds good. Hopefully, this won't take long," I said, running at the three Nephilims. "Good, Gabriel, I want you to be at your best so that human of yours is gone now," Gadreel said. I could see Ziz slowing down, and he was dropping. "Might not be good for you," Gabriel said. *The human's first test. I hope he does well.* He thought

These Nephilims assholes were tearing Ziz apart, and now three of them had nothing better to do than try to get at Gabriel. "Welcome to the show, friends!" I shouted as I tossed myself into the air and crashed, landing on all three of them. I stood up quickly and kick one in the face. He cried out in pain as his two buddies tried to stand. I could hear swords clanking and Ziz cried as I ran over to his right-wing and saw six Nephilims tearing at his flesh. "I got to get them off here," I said to myself as I spotted a sword not far away. "I guess I will have to use this," I said, climbing down. "These Nephilim bastards are all over my wing!" Ziz cried. "Hang on, Ziz, I'm coming!" I shouted. "Never mind me, boy. You must take Gabriel with you and go!" Ziz shouted back. "Boy, my wing will not last much longer. Go!" Ziz boomed. I could hear the sadness in his voice that he knew the same thing I did, he was going to die.

Times have changed him, Gadreel, at one point and time, wasn't known for his fighting. Two thousand years give him a long time to work on it. "Brother, you got soft in these years," Gadreel said. Gabriel had hope that I would stay away until the fight was over, but that's how hope works, sometimes bad. "I will peel the flesh from your bones, brother," Gadreel said. Gabriel looked behind him to see me pop up, and I pointed to Ziz and gave a neck-cutting motion as I pointed out into the distance. *Good, the human knows that Ziz is finished and that we might have to jump,* he thought. *Good, Freddie will get off first, and I will find him on the ground.* Gabriel saw me run to Ziz's head, taking out two Nephilims as he moved. "You keep worrying about that human. It will be your undoing," Gadreel said, trying to kick Gabriel. He dodged the kick but almost cut across his face. "You are always worried about things you shouldn't be," Gadreel said. Gabriel had good reasons to worry about me, and based on what Michael said, they all should be.

Michael stood across from Gabriel as Uriel got ready to meet Jophiel. From what Gabriel heard, I had a close call in the desert and needed something for me to wear. "I could only wonder what Jophiel is doing out there," Gabriel said. "Jophiel believes that the boy is the *Redeemer*," Michael said back to Gabriel. "What? That's impossible. There hasn't been a Redeemer since Peter," I disagreed. Both Raphael and Chamuel looked over at Gabriel as he leaned in closer to them. "Has anyone told the human about this? This might be something he needs to know about," I said. "Jophiel said not to tell him yet, but I will tell you this, brother, you will come face to face Gadreel. If the human saves your life, then it will be like what brother Jophiel said," Michael said. "I hope you are wrong, brother," Gabriel responded.

I ran to the top of Ziz's head and looked out onto the mountains, which were nothing more than a vast gravel pit. It went on for about a thousand meters until a group of trees appeared suddenly under us. "Well, this is like jumping out of a perfect airplane. But this plane is alive and could talk," I said. I looked back to Gabriel who was still fighting the fallen angel, and I didn't want to get in his way till I saw a way out. I looked down to see more and more trees popping out of the mist. "This might be the best place to jump, I guess," I said to myself as I saw Gabriel slowly fighting his way to me. "Good, by the time he gets up here, we need to be ready to jump and hope all these Nephilim jokers go down with the ship," I said to myself. Ziz was trying to get over the mountain, and I heard something. I suddenly hit Ziz hard as Gabriel and the fallen angel were thrown up to where I was. Gabriel's sword flew from his hands, and he hit Ziz's back as the fallen brought something out in his left hand. "Gabriel, look out!" I shouted. Gabriel faced the fallen as something hit his chest, and he fell down. Gabriel was holding his chest as he fell off Ziz. I jumped up and ran off Ziz, too, pushing off the back of his neck as I held my hand out to reach

Gabriel. I saw that the fallen angel threw something at me…it was his sword. "Fuck," I murmured. I tried to turn in the air and the blade just barely missed my stomach by an inch. I fell to Gabriel and grabbed him. As we descended into the trees, a loud boom sound was the last thing I remembered.

Sacred Prostitution

Ziz fell from the sky and hit the last standing mountain as Gadreel floated over. "I missed that damn human," Gadreel said. He was looking down into the trees where I and Gabriel had landed. Gadreel watched as the Nephilims were now working on Ziz's body, tearing large pieces of flesh from him. Finally, Yeqon flew over at him. "Is everything okay?" he asked. "Go down there and find Gabriel," Gadreel answered, pointing to the trees. "Yes," Yeqon said, floating down to the ground. "All that work, brother, will come undone," Gadreel said murmured.

    I opened my eyes and saw that something was getting closer to us. "Fuck," I whispered and looked around to see Gabriel propped up by a tree. "Gabriel, we need to go," I whispered. I stopped when I saw what was stuck in his chest. It looked like some kind of tree root coming out of his chest. I had no idea what to do, and I had a feeling that I couldn't help him. Hell, even if I wanted to, I wouldn't have the time. I picked Gabriel up and helped him stand. "You...must...leave me," he stuttered. "Fuck, that's...Just walk, okay?" I snapped as I helped him along. "Jophiel. Jophiel, I need some help," I whispered. A voice filled my head as we walked around another tree. "Freddie, what is wrong?" Jophiel asked. I could tell that Jophiel was worried just by the sound of his voice. "I'm fine, but Gabriel got stabbed," I whispered. I turned around and saw that the angel was already standing where we landed. "Stabbed? Gabriel? What does the blade look like?" Jophiel asked.

"Red, almost like a tree root coming out of the right side of his chest," I answered. The shock was in his voice when he asked me that question. "The Root of Evil. They must have got it from the Forest of Suicide," he said. "Can I help him?" I asked. "No, once you are stabbed by the Root of Evil, there is no help that I know of. Listen to me, Freddie, he's going to change slowly until…." Jophiel said, stopping short. "Until what?" I snapped. I had to hide behind a tree as the angel started to fly our way. "….he will become a Fallen, and all the work he has done will be undone," Jophiel answered. "I have another problem. A Fallen is following us. Can I stop him?" I questioned. "Yes, but you're going to need Gabriel's sword," Jophiel answered. I looked down to his waist and saw that his sword was gone. "Jophiel, I'm going to need another plan. He doesn't have his sword. He must have lost it during the fight," I said. "You're going to have to get Gabriel to call his sword," Jophiel said. I looked down at Gabriel. "There's no way he can call the sword, while there are two of these assholes around," I said. "Once you have the sword, you can injure any of the Fallen, or kill, if you wish," Jophiel said. "Well, I'm not so sure about that," I whispered. Jophiel said nothing to this either because he knew there's nothing else he can do to help me. "Now, I have to get Gabriel to call his sword," I murmured to myself.

Gabriel's body wasn't holding up with the root inside his chest. "Freddie, you're going to have to leave me here," he said. "Enough of that talk. I need you to call your sword," I explained. "I will try," he answered, holding my hand to the sky. Lightning hit Gabriel's hand, and then his sword appeared. "I'm going to have to take care of this guy," I told myself. Gabriel looked over at me thinking to stop me from what I'm about to do, until the pain started to crawl from his chest spreading all throughout his body. "So, it's true, a human in hell," a fallen said. I could tell from the voice that it was Yeqon. I knew his voice from the moment he started talking. "Yeah, human. What about it, friend?" I asked. "I will rip out your throat, human," Yeqon said. I moved slowly to the left as Yeqon moved slowly towards me. Gabriel wanted to tear the root from his chest, but that would mean he would die and I would be alone. Looking at things now, we were more than likely going to die here anyway. Gabriel tried to stand, but his legs weren't working, and he had to use the tree behind him for balance. "Looks like Gabriel is not holding up well," Yeqon teased. I didn't look back at Gabriel, I didn't take my eyes off Yeqon. "Good, he knows you're dangerous with the sword. Keep him on the defense and don't give him anything," I whispered to myself. Yeqon struck, attacking me with his blade. It missed, and I tried to stab him but only to manage to cut his arm just above the elbow. "Human bastard!" Yeqon shouted and came at me this time from above. I rolled out of the way and jumped back as Yeqon turned back to me. "You think you can fight me, mortal? You will fail, your human kind has always failed!" Yeqon snapped. I said nothing, only preparing myself for the next attack. *Good Freddie, wait for an open, then you might be able to live through this*, Gabriel thought.

The asshole was strong, but he waited too long to attack, and he liked to hear himself talk. For some reason, I hated the word human, just the sound of the word pissed me off. I don't know what's going on, but I know I can't rush anything, and Gabriel needed help. "Don't tell me this human doesn't like to talk," he said. The angel in front of me looked just as evil as his friend I saw jumping from Ziz. The only difference was that he looked like an Asian, just a shade darker. He attacked again, and this time I rolled to the left, and he followed. Our blades clashed, sending sparks out from both blades. This time we were face to face, and he tried to head-butt me. He hit me in the face as I kicked him in the leg. He cried out in pain. "Enough of this, mortal! I'm done playing nice with you," he said and reached out to grabbed me. I moved to the left, and he got nothing but air. I rolled back to get some distance from him, and I saw something leave his hand and came flying through the air at my face. I dropped down and saw him flying at me, hugging the ground as he grabbed my right hand, knocking the sword from my hand. He held me in the air with a big smile on his face. "So, human, any last words before I cut out your heart?" he asked. I smiled at him. I'm sorry but I just couldn't help myself. "What is so funny, mortal?!" he snapped. I looked over at him, "Gabriel," I said. Suddenly from below him came Gabriel, cutting him like a hot dog bun. I dropped to the ground, covered in a black liquid like oil but thicker, almost like molasses. "Nice save Gabriel," I whispered. I looked over at him, and he was on the ground trying to pull himself up. "I will…be unable…to do…that again, Freddie," Gabriel stuttered. "We need to get you some help," I said. I picked him up, and he handed me his sword, "You might need it," I said. "You will…need…it more if…this root takes…control of me," Gabriel stuttered. I started walking off, holding Gabriel up as we left. "I hope Jophiel has a plan," I said to myself.

Jophiel walked over to Michael, who was sitting under a tree next to the house. "Is everything okay?" Michael asked. "We have a problem," Jophiel answered. Michael stood up and looked over to Jophiel. "Is it the human?" Michael asked. "No, Gabriel was stabbed with a piece of the Root of Evil," Jophiel whispered. "What?!" Michael snapped. Jophiel held up a hand to stop Michael from yelling too loud. "I'm going to send the human to her," Jophiel whispered. Michael looked over to him with a look of part shock and part amazement. "Are you sure? That woman would care less for us?" Michael said. Jophiel looked over to the house. "I know, but the human is smart, and it's just as you said it would happen," Jophiel said. "The human might be smart, but this woman is a demon, and not just any demon, the first wife of Adam. She might outsmart him," Michael said. "I know, but if he can get him to her, then there might be a shot to help our brother," Jophiel explained. Uriel came outside and waved to both of them as she walked around the house. "It must be the human's choice to take him there. We can't make him," Michael said. "Freddie has a loyalty about him which is an odd trait, and so far, he has not failed yet," Jophiel said. "I'm not saying that the human is weak. From what you have told me, he is a strong human of mind and body, but this isn't an enemy he will be able to defeat, it's Lilith," Michael said. "Trust in Freddie. He is somebody here," Jophiel said. Michael said nothing as Jophiel walked away from him, talking, "I hope you are right, Jophiel," Michael said.

Meanwhile, Gadreel floated down to see what was going on. He had heard the sounds of sword clashing, then suddenly became quiet. *What are you doing down there, brother?* He said to himself. He landed next to a tree and started looking around. "Yeqon, brother, where are you?!" Gadreel shouted. He walked down a small hill and saw Yeqon. He was cut in half, and his blood covered the fallen tree next to his body. "Damn you, Gabriel, damn you and that fucking monkey of yours!" he shouted. "When I find you, I'm going to kill you slowly!" Gadreel added.

We had made it up on a large hill, only falling twice when a voice cut through the silence. I could only make out bits and pieces of what was said. "Gabriel, damn you…." and there was something about a monkey. "What the hell was that?" I asked. "It's Gadreel…you did…kill his…brother," Gabriel said who sounded so weak already. "His brother was a real asshole, so I'm not too broke up about that," I said. Gabriel smiled as we hid behind a tree. "Can he smell us?" I asked. "No…." Gabriel answered. "Good, because we're in trouble here," I said. I kept looking around for a good hiding place until Gadreel finally took off. "Freddie, are you still with us, friend?" a voice asked. "Yes, Jophiel, I'm here," I answered. "You're going to have to take him to a small castle not far from you," Jophiel said. "Okay, will the people there be able to fix him?" I asked. "Maybe, and they're not people. They're demons, so you must be on your guard," Jophiel answered. "Demons? Fuck my life, Jophiel. Couldn't one of you fix him?" I asked again. "No, and even if we could, it would take too long. Focus on me, Freddie. Do not listen to anything Gabriel says from here on out, understand?" Jophiel asked. "I got it," I answered, looking up to the sky. Great, now I'm stuck with an angel that might turn on me. Better get him to these demons and hope they can fix him. I looked around and ran to the next tree. As a gust of wind nearly blew me down, I had to take cover behind a fallen log as a shadow fell over the trees. "Fuck," I murmured, as the shadow came closer to us. "God, Creator, if you're up there, I could use some help," I whispered. "You will not hide from me, Gabriel. You and your little pet will share the same grave!" the voice shouted. "Gabriel, buddy, stay here. I'll lead him away from us the better way I can," I said. "No, I will do it," Gabriel said. I remember what Jophiel said earlier. I should not trust anything Gabriel said. *Thanks a lot, Jophiel*, I whispered. I looked over to Gabriel and knew he couldn't get ten steps without dropping in pain, and the color in his was all but gone. "I'm going to do it. You just sit here and stay quiet," I snapped. Gabriel looked at me as if I told his mother to go fuck herself. "I see. So, you talked with Jophiel. Good. Listen to what he tells you," Gabriel whispered. I watched the tree in front of him and saw that the shadow had moved to the right. That's when I shot out of the hiding place like a bat out of hell. I could hear a voice scream out as I ran behind a tree and took off downhill.

I took off, stopping for only a second behind a tree before taking off again. Gabriel wanted to help me, but his body just wasn't moving right. To make matters worse, the voices started up. "Kill the human, murder that monkey!". Gabriel hoped that I will return quickly. Otherwise, he will be doomed. Gabriel could hear a loud boom fill the forest. "Damn this thing," he said. He tried to stand, but there was nothing left for him to use. *If Freddie uses the great light, then he might stand a chance against him*, Gabriel said to himself.

I was ducking through the trees as the angel was giving chase. I could hear something falling down behind me as I powered over a log and behind another tree. I looked back to see the angel fire something from his blade. I ducked out of the way. The tree exploded into splinters as I ran to what was the edge of a cliff. *Shit. I didn't think I would be this close to the end*, I said to myself as I ran. I need a plan and I must be quick, otherwise, I would be in trouble by the end. *I could try to jump it*, I said to myself. The human side of me saw the drop-off and told me to fuck that shit and stop. The cliff was coming up fast. "Fuck it! fuck it!" I shouted and jumped as the edge came rushing up. I threw myself into the air and found out two things. One, what goes up must come down, and two, the power was very, very incredible. I could feel the air under my feet, and I saw the other side come up to me and had to roll as I hit the other side and rolled to a stop, hitting a tree. "Damn," I murmured. I looked over to the angel, stopped, and floated on the other side. "Well, human, you must have the Power," he said. I said nothing to him as I ducked out of sight. "Get back here, human. You fool!" he shouted. "This bastard needs a hobby or a wife one," I said, taking off again. I ducked into a log crawling inside as he flew overhead. "This will buy me some time," I said. A shadow flew overhead as I crawl to the other side. "I hope Gabriel is doing better than me right now," I murmured.

Gabriel could barely stand as he tried to walk through the woods. He could hear Gadreel yelling and screaming about something, but he was too far away to hear anything. *I hope Freddie is okay*, I said to myself. The voices returned. "Kill the human! Tell Gadreel where he is." Gabriel shook the cobwebs out of his head and kept walking until he saw a cliff. "Freddie…where…are…you?" I murmured. He saw Gadreel flying around the ridge. *I better use this chance to get rid of him,* He thought, looking over to the other side. He readied himself with the last weapon he had.

Waiting inside the log felt like years. So I would have to come out and face the guy, and then I would be in trouble. I poked my head out slowly and saw that he was still in the sky looking for me. "This guy doesn't have a home to go to," I murmured under my breath. I looked over to the cliff on the other side and saw Gabriel pointing something up in the sky at the angel. "What's he doing?" I said as Gabriel kept his eyes on the angel in the sky. I looked out to see the angel in the sky looking down at me and pointing. "There you are, monkey," he said, floating down to me. I looked just behind him to Gabriel, who now had a bow and an arrow. "Now are you done running so I can destroy you, mortal?" he asked. I said nothing to him as he hovered just above me. Gabriel let the arrow go, and it flew through the air. The angel turned just in time for the golden arrow to hit his right-wing. A sound like scorching meat could be heard, and he fell to the ground holding his wing. "Hey pal, it must suck to be you," I smiled, kicking him down by the cliff. He tried to stand only for me to hit him in the chest with a well-timed kick, and he was sent falling off the ridge to the bottom of the gorge. "Hope you enjoy that landing, asshole!" I shouted. I looked over to Gabriel, who sat down by a tree, "Nice shot!" I shouted. Gabriel said nothing but the smile on his told the tale. After finding enough room to run and jump back, I rejoined Gabriel and helped him to the other side. "Jophiel, are you there? Gadreel is dead, or I hope he is," I said. Jophiel's voice entered my mind. "Good, you're going to have to take him to a small castle not far from you. There you will find Lilith, she is the only one that can help him," Jophiel said. "Can we trust her?" I asked. "No, trust no one at this point until Gabriel is completely healed," Jophiel answered. *Well, there's always that,* I whispered. I helped Gabriel along as we walked into the woods.

After walking for an hour, we came to a castle built into a hillside of black-red rock. "This must be the place," I said, looking over to Gabriel. Gabriel was looking bad, his blue eyes were a menacing red color. "It will not be long now. You might want to keep your distance from me," Gabriel said. The door to the castle was about as big as a dump truck. I tried to look for something to knock it with. I saw a silver door knocker and hit the door three times. "Let's hope that someone is home," I murmured. "What is it, human?" a voice said as it sent a chill down my spine that didn't go too well for the army side of me. "I need some help. Can you help us?" I asked. I waited for an answer and suddenly the doors opened and standing in front of us was a woman and not just any woman. First off, she was wearing all white with a black ring in the center of her chest. Next, the white dress was made out of tissue paper because I saw everything. *If that's their idea of a dress, then we might have problems*, I said under my breath. "Well, what brings you here?" the woman asked. "My friend needs your help. I was told that you could help him," I answered. I wanted to try to be honest and see what would happen. "Right this way," the woman replied. She turned and walked ahead of us, and I tried my best to look at the ground mostly, but that was hard to ask of my army mind. We walked down a long hallway that opened up to a room with three other women sitting around watching as we came in. "What do you have here, Na'amah?" one of the women asked. "Looks like a human, and Gabriel," the woman said. She was the tallest of the four, and just by watching her and I did a lot of that, she was a gorgeous woman. She looked almost like Vida Guerra, just a shade lighter but perfect in nearly every way. The only knock I could give her was a small tall that came out from atop of her butt. "What brings a human and Gabriel to my home?" the woman asked. "I was told that you could help him," I answered. "Why should we, human, if he changes and becomes a fallen, all his works will be undone," the red-headed woman said. "So, you're just going to let him change? Some fucking prostitution this is!" I snapped. "You gave it a tried, Freddie, your just going to have to go on without me," Gabriel said, looking up to me. "Okay, what will it take to help him if you could? I bet you can't help him anyway," I said. I looked down to Gabriel, who gave me the *what the fuck are you doing* look. "Human, I would gut you for saying such things," the redhead said. "You doubt our power? Tell me, what do they call you on earth?" she asked. "Freddie, and you are?" I questioned back. "I'm Lilith, honey, and you're a long way from home," she said. "Well, do the rest of the ladies have a name?" I asked. "The one you followed is Na'amah, and the redhead goes by Eisheth Zenunim. The quiet one there is Agrat Bat Mahlat," Lilith said. "Can you save my friend or not?" I asked. "I will save this angel, but you will give me something in return," Lilith answered. I was thinking the whole time, hoping that it wasn't my soul. "You will take me to bed while my sisters heal your angel," Lilith said. For a moment, I think my jaw hit the stone floor. "What?!" I said. "That is the only way we will have business with you, human," Lilith said. I looked over to Gabriel, who gave the *don't do it, you fool* look. "Okay, as long as you don't kill him, and he'll be okay," I said. "Yes, now follow me," Lilith said. I looked back at Gabriel as the three other women picked him up and took him away.

Lilith led the way as we walked down a well-lit hallway. "I hate to ask, but where are we going?" I asked. "My room," Lilith answered. I started to sweat a little, this would be the first time I could say I slept with a demon in the history of my life. She came to a stop in front of a wooden door and turned the knob. Inside I saw nothing but red and black colored bed sheets and cloth hanging from the ceiling. "Nice room," I grinned. "Glad you like it. Most of this came from your world with a little from hell," Lilith said. Lilith walked over to her bed and laid down, "Come over here, human, and get close to me," she said, pointing to the space next to her. I walked over and sat down, and before I could take anything off, she wrapped her arms around me. "I know it was you who took the Great Power. You have to take some great mind to do that," Lilith whispered into my ear. I looked over to her and saw that her eyes had gotten big, about as big as a baseball. "I guess I should have said to stay human," I joked, trying to smile. "Don't worry, human, this is the only change I can take," she said, pulling me down with her. She was sniffing the air as she got on top of me. "You haven't been with too many women in your world, have you?" she asked. I could feel myself turning red at the question. "Well, I have a girlfriend, and yes, we have done that kind of stuff," I blurted out. "Good, but I'm going to have to ask you to forget her while you're with me, okay?" Lilith asked. I said nothing, maybe because she was taking off her tissue paper-like dress by then.

Gabriel woke to two women standing over him. "Gabriel, always good to see you," one of the women said. "Na'amah, where's Freddie?" he asked. "Don't worry about that human, he is busy," she said as a woman scream could be heard. "I told that boy not to do this," Gabriel said. "If I were you, I would hold still, angel, this may hurt a little," Na'amah said, putting a grey cream on the Root of Evil. Gabriel could feel it burning his skin as they watched. "Agrat, bring me that knife. I'm going to have to cut part of this off before we can go forward," Na'amah said. Gabriel couldn't see what was going on; he was lying on a bed, and from what he could see, another woman was standing in the dark. "If you're going to hide from my sight, you can at least do something with that hair of yours, Eisheth," Gabriel said. "Sorry, Gabriel, you never liked redheads," Eisheth said, walking over to his side. Na'amah nodded as both she and Agrat left the room, leaving Gabriel with Eisheth. "So, what now?" Gabriel asked. "I'm going to fix you just like my sister said she would, but first, I and you must have a talk about the human," Eisheth said. "I guess I have no choice but to tell you, or you will let me die," Gabriel said. "No, I just wish to know what is the mighty Gabriel doing walking around Hell with a human," Eisheth said. "You know I can't tell you, Eisheth," Gabriel answered. "I remember the nights that you would hold me in your arms," Eisheth said, putting her hand on Gabriel's face. "I know only that the human must return to his world soon," Gabriel said. "Fine, keep your secrets. Just remember who saved your life, Gabriel," Eisheth said as she took hold of the root. "I will be able to pull this thing out once Na'amah returns and starts the show," Eisheth whispered. *I hope that Freddie is holding up better than me*, I murmured.

"Damn it!" I shouted as Lilith dug her long fingernails into my skin. I looked at her, and I saw that she wasn't clawing at my skin, she was clawing at my very soul. "I forgot what it's like having a human soul around," Lilith smirked. She clawed again at my body, and a white kind of dust came out "I guess it's too late to ask for some painless non-soul scratching sex," I snapped, grabbing hold of her hands. "You agreed to this, and I'm just enjoying every second of it," Lilith said. I rolled her over on her back and pinned her hands above her head. "Oh, so, what are you going to do with me now?!" she asked with a smile on her face. "We're going to do this the human way," I smiled. "Okay, what is this… human way?" she asked. I kissed her neck and then started to suck on it. "What was that?!" she said with her large expressive eyes looking into mine. She grabbed the top of my head. "It's called a hickey," I smiled. She smiled at me. "Show me more of this human…way," Lilith said, kissing my lips.

Na'amah returned, only this time she was naked and had Agrat with her. "Just to let you know, angel, we have to touch your flesh to get this root out," Na'amah said. Gabriel said nothing and only nodded as Na'amah sat next to him, mixing something in a small bowl before getting on top of him. "This is going to take some time, so you might want to relax," Na'amah said. She touched his skin and could feel the heat from her hand and body, she rubbed the black-gold ooze on his chest, around where the root was. "Eisheth, the human is a *Redeemer*," Gabriel revealed. Eisheth, Na'amah, and Agrat looked at me with a look of shock, "Impossible, there hasn't been a Redeemer since Peter, and he's dead now!" Eisheth exclaimed, stepping forward. Na'amah kept working on the root as Gabriel spoke. "Freddie showed up at Jophiel's home just like Peter did so long along," Gabriel explained. "Does the human know about this?" Eisheth asked. "No. Michael said he wasn't ready to know it yet," Gabriel answered. Eisheth said nothing as Na'amah put her hand up to the root and slowly started to pull it out. "What is she doing?" Gabriel asked, changing the topic. "Na'amah is taking it out slowly. At some point, we'll have to get you some Holy Water from Lilith. But by the sound of those two, they won't be done for a while," Eisheth smiled. "I guess humans in his world have something for demons," Gabriel said. "Well, most of them are children of our...so they just might have learned a thing or two," Eisheth smiled. Eisheth turned and walked to the door. "I'm going to ask for the Holy Water, with some hope that she might break away for a moment," Eisheth said, walking out of the room.

Gadreel awoke to a shadow standing over him. "So, you've come to take my soul, Azazel?" Gadreel asked. "Shut the fuck up! Where is the mortal?" Azazel questioned back. "I don't know. They attacked me and took off somewhere," Gadreel answered. "Fucking useless!" Azazel snapped. "Oh, if you think you can do a better job, I would like to see it," Gadreel grinned. Azazel said nothing to this as Nimrod walked up. "Are you okay?" he asked. "I can't fly. I must call the others to help us," Gadreel answered. "You call whoever you want. I'm going after them before they get away," Azazel said, taking to the sky. "Hey...." Nimrod says until Gadreel cuts him off. "Don't stop him. Just let him be. He always wants to do it his own way," Gadreel said. "In the meantime, help me up, and we'll call the others," Gadreel added. Nimrod picked Gadreel up off the ground and saw that he was covered in mud. "Are you sure you don't need something to wipe your face with?" Nimrod asked. "No, this is the fun part…the chase," Gadreel answered with a sick smile.

I woke to a smack on the face, "Oh! What did I do?" I asked. Lilith smiled at me, "This is prostitution, not a hotel. That will cost you a little more," Lilith smiled. "I don't think I can pay for that type of stay," I said, getting out of the bed. A knock came on the door. "Lilith, I need the Holy Water," a voice said. "Yes, Eisheth, hang on," Lilith answered. I watched as Lilith walked over to a closet next to the bed and pulled out a glass bottle filled with some kind of green water. She walked over to the door and opened it and waiting there was Eisheth. "Thanks, we're ready for the final part to heal his little angel friend," Eisheth said, looking at me. "Good. Freddie, if you follow Eisheth, she will take you to Gabriel," Lilith said. I put my shirt on and walked out behind Eisheth down the hallway to the open room. "How is Gabriel?" I asked. Eisheth cut her eyes at me before answering. "Fine, I think he wanted you to leave him, but you brought him here. How did you know about this place, human?" Eisheth asked. "I had some help," I explained. She said nothing to this as we crossed the room and came to a stop in front of a wooden door. She opened it, and lying there on the bed was Gabriel, and on top of him was Na'amah. "Did we walk in on something?!" I said, feeling a little red on the face. Gabriel looked over at me. "If I knew you had an alone time, I would have waited," I smiled. "No, Freddie, it's just part of what they must do to help me get this out," Gabriel murmured. I looked at the root, and it had changed color from red to dark brown. "Is that a good thing?" I asked. "Changing color is a good thing. Now comes the hard part," Na'amah said as Lilith walked in. "Now she has to pull the root out and pour the Holy Water into the wound so it will close," Lilith said, standing next to me. There was something about Lilith that I couldn't place. Almost like a friend with benefits, you can love and watch a movie at the same time. I looked over to Eisheth, who had a look on her face like she wanted to tell me something but she couldn't. "Is there anything I can do to help?" I asked. "Well, that's a first. A helpful human," Na'amah grinned. I said nothing to this only because I'm the only human that might have went to hell, still trying to figure out if this is a good thing or not. "Now, human, the hard part begins," Lilith said. With that, Na'amah poured the Holy water into the root, and a fizzle sound could be heard. I could see that this was hurting Gabriel. "What's going on?!" I shouted. "Calm down, human. We must first get the root out of his body. Then we can heal him, this is the hard part," Lilith said, resting a hand on my shoulder. The root by this time was small, about a tenth of the size it was before, as Na'amah pulled it out slowly. "Good, now we wait until the wound heals," Na'amah said. I stepped forward and gave a weak smile to Gabriel. "Well, still with us," I said. "Yes, we still need to meet up with Raphael so he can take you on into Aokigahara," Gabriel explained. "You need to rest," I said. "You might not get a chance!" Agrat snapped, looking out the window. I walked over to her and saw something flying through the air. "I hope that's not Gadreel," I murmured. "No, someone worst," Agrat said, running over to Lilith. "It's the Angel of Death," Agrat added. I gave a puzzled look over to Gabriel, who was now trying to stand. "Hell, it's Azazel. I'm in no shape to fight him," Gabriel said, holding himself up. I came over and assisted him. "Don't make me guess. What are we up against?" I asked. "Azazel is the Angel of Death. His power is equal to mine," Gabriel answered. *Great, that means he'll mop the floor with us*, I thought as Lilith grabbed my right arm. "This way!" she said, leading me to the door. "Agrat, get rid of that and get ready for our guest," Lilith said, pointing to the root as we left the room. Lilith led us down the hallway to a hidden door that looked like bookshelves, "This will lead you to Aokigahara and from there you're on your own," Lilith said. "Thank you very much for your help," I said. "You are an odd human, if you end up in Hell again, come see me," Lilith said with a smile. I held Gabriel up as we walked through the doorway. It was short by my standards, but we made it work. "I'll get you home as quick as I can," I said.

    Azazel landed on the steps of the home of Lilith, and welcoming him was Agrat. "I wish to talk with Lilith, woman. So, get her," He said. "Do you mind waiting for a moment until she comes to see you?" Agrat asked. "Hurry," he murmured. Agrat walked back inside and met Lilith out of sight of Azazel. "He's waiting for you," Agrat whispered. Lilith stepped into the doorway as Azazel walked forward. "How can I help the Angel of Death?" Lilith questioned. "There is a human in hell that I think might be here with another. One by the name of Gabriel," Azazel answered. "I'm sorry, but the only one that was here was a demon," Lilith said. "Do you mind if I check the place out?" Azazel asked. "Go on, have fun, Azazel," Lilith answered. Azazel walked through the door, and to his right stood Na'amah and Eisheth. "If you need something, please let me know," Eisheth said. Azazel sniffed the air and took two more steps before turning to Na'amah. "I need some Holy Water if you don't mind," Azazel said. Na'amah nodded and turned away from Azazel, and walked down the hallway. Azazel sniffed the air again before looking at the painting on the wall. "You still have that painting up of Daystar?" Azazel asked. "Yes, he was the first true husband I had," Lilith answered. Na'amah returned with a glass of Holy Water and gave it to Azazel. He drank it slowly at first before finishing off the rest. "I will leave you to your business," Azazel said as he handed the glass to Na'amah. "If you see a human and his angelic friend, please, let me know," Azazel added. Lilith nodded as Azazel walked back down the hallway.

The change in light outside blinded me for a few seconds. I saw that we were standing in front of a forest. "I'm guessing this is the place?" I asked. "Yes, I can sense Raphael. We better find him fast," Gabriel said. *So this is the Forest of Aokigahara, the Forest of Suicide*, I said to myself.

The Forest of Aokigahara

From what I could see, the forest where we at was no different from any other forest I've been to. It was a thick forest, and very little sunlight was hitting the ground. There were even birds singing in the tree tops. "Wait a minute, wait just one damn minute. Every place in hell had something crazy in it, but this place is just like my backyard," I said. "True, this is the only place in hell that you could say is peaceful," Gabriel said. Gabriel stopped as I followed his gaze when I saw someone was walking toward us. "Who's there?!" I snapped. "Easy, human," the voice said. Gabriel smiled. "Good to see you, Raphael," Gabriel said, putting his hand on a tree. "Gabriel, what has happened to you?" Raphael asked. "Some fallen by the name of Gadreel and some other guy named Azazel," I answered. "Azazel, well, brother, when you stick your foot in it, you do it big," Raphael murmured. "Once I send him back, the human, we'll go on our way," Raphael said. I could sense that Raphael was worried about Gadreel and Azazel. Hopefully, we put some distance between them and us, Raphael put his hand out, and a golden light covered Gabriel. I heard thunder, and Gabriel was gone. "Hopefully, no one saw that," I said. "No, but we better get moving just in case," Raphael said. I stood next to him as he pointed off down the road. "We'll have to stay on this road until we get to a lake. Once there, we'll see if Behemoth can take us across," Raphael said. I smiled as we walked down this dirt road.

"How the fuck do you lose them?!" Gadreel shouted. The Nephilims that were listening had their heads down as Azazel floated down to them. A group of Nephilims moved quickly out of the way as he landed. "Nimrod, I see that you made it. You better head to the forest," Azazel said. "They would be fools to go that way," Nimrod said. "They know that, which is why we must find them before they get to Behemoth," Azazel explained. "I'm guessing you couldn't find them either?" Gadreel asked. "For now, they will fuck up, and when they do, I want to be there," Azazel answered. "Sounds good, now we just need them to do something stupid," Nimrod murmured. "That human is a tricky one. We're going to have to make them tip their hand," Gadreel said. "How do we do that?" Nimrod questioned. "To get across the Great Lake of the Damned, they must ride on the mighty Behemoth. We will meet them there and finish this once and for all," Gadreel answered.

Raphael and I walked on the dirt road that cut through the forest. Not knowing if the enemy will jump out and get us kept me on edge like I was in Afghanistan again. "Can you tell me about this place?" I asked. Raphael looked over to me before pointing to one of the trees. "The trees are the souls of people that took their own lives. They must relive that moment every day until the end of days," Raphael answered. "That's nice, I guess," I murmured. "Could be worst. They could be in the Lake of the Damned," Raphael said. "What's that place?" I questioned. "For anyone that takes their own life and fails," Raphael said, looking over to me. "That's fucking nice," I whispered. "What is that word?" Raphael asked. "What word. Nice?" I questioned back. "No, this *fuck* word. I heard humans say that word often, but I have no idea what it means?" Raphael asked. I almost laughed, but I held it back. "Well, it's…a bad word," I explained. "I never got you human. If it's a bad word, why are you using it?" Raphael asked. I felt like a father trying to tell my small child about the birds and the bees. "It means to hit," I said. "So, when you use this word *fuck* you mean to hit someone with it? I still don't get it," Raphael said. I giggled at this as we walked along. "Can you tell me a bit about this…Azazel guy?" I asked. "He's the new Angel of Death," Raphael answered. I could tell that there was more to it, but he didn't want to tell me. "Sounds like this guy is bad news," I murmured. "Not really, just an angel that never followed the rules and took the title from our brother,

Samuel," Raphael said. *I see, so this guy is a two-faced son of a bitch.* "Then we'll have to watch out for him and Gadreel. How nice," I murmured. I looked up into the sky only to trip over a tree root that was on the road. *Friendly Freddie, really graceful,* I said to myself. Raphael helped me to my feet again. "You must watch it, Freddie. This is a dangerous road we're on," Raphael whispered. "Yeah, only dangerous because of my feet," I said. "You don't understand. Just because it's peaceful here that doesn't mean there isn't something evil here," Raphael said. His words sent a chill down my spine. As I turned to my right, I heard the sounds of laughter. "What's that?" I asked, looking to Raphael. Raphael quickly put a finger up to his lips, and this time, the laughter grew louder and closer. "We need to get moving," Raphael whispered. "What's that, a demon?" I asked again, softly. "Sometimes worst than that…the ghost of those that have killed themselves," Raphael answered as we walked. "So, that sounds like something we can handle," I said. "My power could, but then Gadreel would know where we are, and we don't need to fight here," Raphael said. A thick mist started to move across the road and around the trees. "Oh hell, I've seen movies that have shit like this in it," I said. Raphael had a look on his face of anger, I could only wonder what could be going through his mind.

Great, I was hoping that the ghost wouldn't come to us, must be my soul they sense. "Freddie, we're going to need to hurry!" Raphael shouted. I nodded, and we took off down the road at a run. The mist was getting thicker, and soon we wouldn't be able to see anything in front of us. "Is the mist alive?" I asked. "Everything in Aokigahara is alive," Raphael answered. We kept running until the mist became a fog, and I couldn't see anything in front of us anymore. I took a step closer to Raphael as the laughter returned. "Don't make me guess. What are we up against?" I asked. "The forest itself is made with the souls of humans that died by suicide. But this is something eviler, this is made from all the humans that died violently," Raphael answered. "So much for Casper the friendly ghost," I murmured. We were now back to back as the mist was closing in. "I bet you have something that can get us out of here?" I questioned. "Yes, I could get rid of the mist," Raphael answered. "But that would also let Gadreel know where we are, right?" I confirmed. "Yes," Raphael answered. "Then we better save it until we badly need it then," I said.

This human thinks well on his feet too, good to know, Raphael thought. "So, what's the plan?" I asked. Raphael was about to answer until something grabbed his leg. "What is this?!" Raphael shouted. Raphael was lifted into the air and tossed off the road and into the forest.

Raphael was grabbed by what looked like some vines, I tried to watch and see where he landed, but soon I was caught too. "Fuck my life! This is just great, Raphael!" I shouted. I heard a voice answered back, followed by a peal of laughter in my left. "Alright, Casper, let's meet face to face," I murmured. "Freddie!" I heard. "Raphael, something is running around here!" I yelled. *Damn, this fog is as thick as a pea soup*, I whispered to myself. What could this thing be, and how could we stop it?

Gadreel stood on a dirt road as three shadows joined him. "Hello, brother, I heard you need help," one shadow said. "Yes, sister, you could say that" Gadreel smiled. "So, how can we help you?" the tallest shadow said. "I need you to find a human who is here in hell and find the angel with him," Gadreel answered. "A human, here, in hell? This human must be lost," another shadow laughed. "Where are they, brother?" the tallest shadow asked. "In Aokigahara would be my guess. They couldn't move that fast. Gabriel was hurt the last time I saw him," Gadreel answered. "Gabriel, here, in hell? It would be so nice to see another brother again after all these years," another shadow said. "Once you find them, bring them to me so I can get my revenge on Gabriel," Gadreel said. "Not a problem, brother. It shall be done," the tallest shadow said. The three of them took off into the air as Nimrod walked over to him. "You should have them soon, Gadreel," Nimrod said. "Yes, but nothing in hell is free or easy," Gadreel murmured.

Raphael stood up again and heard someone laughing, and this time it sounded like it was behind him. By the sound of my voice, I was still on the road, *good*, Raphael thought. "Raphael, something is in the fog, I don't know what, but this fog is indeed alive!" I shouted. *Good, Freddie knows the same thing I just found out*, Raphael said to himself. "Freddie, stay where you are! I will come to you!" Raphael shouted. "Sure thing, not like I can go anywhere! Can't see a damn thing in this stuff!" I called back. We will be able to go no further unless we get that damn hammer. Raphael stood up and saw that he wasn't far from the road and quickly ran back up on it. "Is that you, Raphael?!" I asked with a loud voice.

I waved at him. "Okay, now I know it's you," I said. I walked over to Raphael and looked around. "Please tell me we can get rid of this fog," I pleaded. "Yes, but we'll have to find the Hammer of the Damned. It will be the only way to dispel this fog," Raphael explained. "Sounds good. Where do we start looking?" I asked. "The only place I dare not go...The Demonic Church," Raphael answered, looking over to me. "Church? Man! I haven't been in one of those for some time now," I murmured. Raphael wasn't sure whether I was joking using human sarcasm or if I was being serious. In either case, we'll have to come face to face with one of the Princes of Hell. Something that we might not see through to the end if we can't do something about the fog.

Azazel landed and could hear the laughing of the damned all around him. "Someone must be in the forest for the fog to be this thick," Azazel said to himself. *It seems that you just got here, brother.* Azazel looked up and saw Gadreel and three other fallen floated down to him. "You think this human and our kin will be this much trouble?" Azazel asked. Gadreel smiled. "You can never be too careful, and with the death of Yeqon, I want to catch them quickly," Gadreel answered. Azazel said nothing to this, he only nodded as Gadreel looked over to the other three. "Get rid of this fog and find them," Gadreel said. Azazel watched, not saying a word. As the other three fallen floated back into the air and took off one flew high into the sky. He clapped his hands together and the fog in the area went away. "Good, now the hunt can continue," Gadreel said with a smile.

I was still somewhat surprised that there was a church in hell, even more, surprised that we were heading there. "So, what will we find there?" I asked. Raphael was strolling to not leave me behind. "There is a weapon there that will clean this fog out and knock down this forest," Raphael answered. "Wow, a weapon like that must be guarded closely by someone," I said. Raphael looked back at me. "The weapon belongs to one of the Princes of Hell," Raphael answered. "Great, hard work coming," I murmured. As we passed a group of trees, a gust of wind came through that cleared the fog out. "What the hell was that?!" I shouted. Raphael looked around and quickly pointed to the fallen tree to our right. "Hide, quickly!" Raphael snapped. We ran to the tree, and I saw a small hole just under the left side. "I'm guessing they're on to us?" I questioned. "If you mean that our enemy has come for us, then yes," Raphael answered. "Better cheese it!" I said. "What is this word? This cheese," Raphael asked. "It means to leave, get the fuck out of dodge. A nice way to say that we're running away," I answered. "Oh, I see," Raphael said as we made our way through the trees. The laughing moved with us almost as if it was following us. "I have a feeling we're being tailed," I whispered. Raphael looked over at me. "What's this word…tail?" Raphael asked. I looked back at him with an *are you kidding me* look. "It means someone is following us. Come on, man!" I snapped. We kept running through the forest until we came to a small opening and saw something floating in the sky. "Get down!" I snapped again and pulled Raphael to the ground next to me. "What do you see?" he whispered back. "Something is floating in the sky above us. Might be one of our good friends," I said. "I can sense a strong demonic presence close by," Raphael whispered. "So, we're close to this hammer, I'm guessing?" I asked. "Yes, but if we are seen, then this plan of ours will be for nothing," Raphael answered. I nodded as the shadow floated past us and continue ahead of us.

I have a strong feeling whoever is causing this fog, will be there at that church. I stood up as Raphael tapped my shoulder and point ahead of us. I have understood what he's trying to say because I started walking with him as we both hid behind a tree. Another laugh echoed around us as we made our way slowly through the fog, making sure not to make a sound. "Do you know who's doing this?" I asked Raphael. "I guess one of the princes of hell named Mammon," he answered. I looked over to Raphael as we passed a tree. "So, what's this guy like?" I asked again. "Mammon is the brother of Lucifer and half-brother of the strongest of the prince, Astaroth," Raphael answered. "Oh, well, at least he's in good company, I guess," I said. "Can we talk with him from here?" I added. "No, we would have to get closer to him, and by then, we'll be face to face with him, and that is never good," Raphael answered. "Do demons have a code or a set of beliefs?" I asked. Raphael wondered why I was asking these things. "I guess, but it's nothing like your human honor. These demons respect power. If you have the power, then you get to make the rules," Raphael explained. "Really. That's good to know," I replied.

We came to a creek that was just off to our left. We ran into a lake that smelled of honey and a kind of tea. "What is that smell?" I questioned. Raphael looked over at me. "We're close to the church," he answered. I looked around and couldn't see a damn thing. If the church was close, it must be small. "What are we looking for in a small building?" I asked. "You can't miss it, Freddie. The church is large," Raphael answered. I looked over at him with a puzzled look on my face. "Okay, if you say so," I murmured. We walked along the lake until a stone path appeared in front of us. "I'm guessing this must be the place," I said. Raphael took two steps in front of me. "It's right in front of us. Hopefully, Mammon will be in a good mood to help us," Raphael murmured. We started walking down the path, and as we walked, a large wall began to appear before us. "Damn, you weren't kidding. This building is fucking huge," I said. "There, your human word again…*fuck*. I'm still at a loss as to how you use that word," Raphael said. I smiled a weak smile at him as we came to a small door. "I'm guessing we're taking the side entrance," I smiled. "We must be careful. We are about to enter the home of a powerful demon," Raphael explained. I opened the door and was hit with a rotten smell, unlike anything I've ever smelled before. "It smells like something or someone died in here," I stuttered. "He must be inside then," Raphael whispered. "Then after you, my friend," I said, stepping out of the way. Raphael stepped inside, and I followed close behind as we entered the demonic church.

Mammon, Prince of Hell

I stepped inside the demonic church, and the first thing I felt was that the air was heavy and cloudy. "What's with the air?" I gasped. Raphael came over to me and put his arm around my neck. "The air is a mix of ash and dust from the demons that came before us," Raphael explained. "Great. So, where is this Mammon at?" I questioned. Raphael pointed down the gold brick walkway that we now stood on. "He's at the end of this," Raphael answered. "Down the yellow brick road, I guess," I said. "What?" Raphael said, looking over at me. "Nothing, it's from a human movie," I answered. We walked down the walkway, and the first thing I saw was a statue of five things I guess you could call them. One I knew was the Lord of the Flies, but the others, I had no idea who they were. "Whoa! What is that?" I asked. "That is the statues of the Princes. Every demon that came here prayed to all of them," Raphael explained. These five statues were placed around the room we were in. At the center of the room was a cross just like in a church on Earth. There was a significant difference though, the cross was displayed upside down. As I got closer, the floor under this cross had a large hole. I couldn't see what was down in the hole because of the ash and dust, but I could see that Raphael had stopped. "Is there something wrong?" I asked. "This is as close as I can get," he said, holding his chest. "Then I'll go down there," I said, hopping down into the hole. I slid to the bottom of the hole, and on the cross, I saw something tied to it upside down. "What the hell," I said to myself as I walked over to it. Suddenly my skin peeled away from my body, like something you would see in a lava lamp. I fell to the ground as a voice spoke out. *I wonder who you are. You must be stronger than most humans*, I was looking around to see who's talking. My eyes came to rest on the thing that was tied to the cross. Looking back at me were four eyes that seemed to float around where the head was. "I'm guessing you are Mammon...." I coughed. Each eye was red with a hint of green in them. "I'm surprised that a mortal can get this close to me, most would burst into flames," Mammon said. "I'm a special mortal," I said. "That is true. I can tell, *Redeemer*" Mammon smiled. I took a knee as a mouth appeared filled with sharp teeth. "Why do you call me Redeemer?" I asked. "You don't even know why you're here, human? They must not have told you yet," Mammon answered. "The Redeemer is a human that will save mankind in its darkest hour. You will stand against the enemy of Creator and bring about the Change," Mammon added. "Okay, let me ask you another question. How does a Prince of Hell get tied to a cross in a church?" I asked. Mammon laughed, a deep laugh, the same laugh that I heard in the forest. "I was tied here by Azazel, if I could get my hands on him, I would spit on him as I'm peeling his wings off," Mammon answered. I looked at him tied to the cross, there were chains, rope, and some kind of lock that everything ran out of. "What if I tell you that Azazel is here, outside this very building," I said. Mammon looked at me. His eyes had a look in them that I've seen before, a look of revenge.

I was down in that hole for a while, and Raphael couldn't hear what was going on. *I hope he's okay*, he said to himself. Raphael heard footsteps and turned down the golden brick walkway to see the fog slowly disappear. He turned back to see me stepping out of the hole. "Are you okay?" Raphael asked. "Yeah, just met Mammon. Nice guy, by the way," I answered. Raphael still doesn't get why humans use sarcasm at times even if their lives are in danger already. "I have a plan, but you might not like it," I smiled. "What is this plan that you think I won't like?" Raphael questioned back. "He hates Azazel. We could use that to send him against him, which would buy us some time," I explained. Raphael looked at me wondering if I have lost all sense. "You want to free a Prince of Hell and hope he doesn't kill us? Freddie, you are crazy... smart, but crazy," Raphael said. "Well, you got a better idea? I'm open for suggestions," I murmured. I had a good point, and if Mammon killed one or two of them, they might not try to stop us again. "How can we free him?" Raphael asked. A smile came to my face as I pointed to the top of the cross, "I knew this might be a bad idea," Raphael said, putting his hands on his face.

Well, sometimes, my plans have a way of coming undone, but I blame that on Afghanistan. I told Raphael, pointing to the top of the cross, that it will free Mammon if we knock it down. From the look on Raphael's face, he didn't want to believe it. "Did he tell you this, or were you the one who really thought about this?" Raphael questioned. "Well, he didn't tell me this, but yes, that's what I was thinking," I answered. Raphael again put his hands on his face. "So, he didn't tell you this? Are you sure?" Raphael asked. I looked at him a long while before answering, "Believe me, I am sure," I replied. Raphael looked to the top of the cross. "It could be possible, but we would need the hammer to break these chains," Raphael explained. "Good, so we find this hammer and come back. Then free him so he can get his revenge on Azazel, and we can keep running for our lives," I said. "I'm glad, Freddie, that this plan to you seems easy!" Raphael snapped. "No, I think Murphy will come along and fuck this plan up, I know Murphy," I said with a smile. "Who is this Murphy, another enemy that you and Gabriel crossed?" Raphael asked. "No, Murphy's Law, we have it in the army. Anything that can go wrong will go wrong and fast," I answered. "Then pray we don't cross this Murphy, human. He sounds like an unforgiving demon," Raphael said. I laughed at that. I guess angels don't have Murphy's Law up there in heaven.

Behemoth

I stood next to Raphael as we waited at the door to ensure that no Fallen were coming. We stepped out to the fog, which had gotten thicker since the last time we were outside. "Do you know where this hammer is?" I asked. "No, but we may have to cross the lake. It's in a castle on the island," Raphael answered. "I hope there's a boat that goes out there," I whispered. *Humans and their sarcasm. I still don't understand it*, Raphael thought. "We will have to ride Behemoth to get there," Raphael said. "Behemoth? What is that?" I asked. "The great land monster that will come when your world ends. We may have to wait for him," Raphael explained. "I take it you guys don't talk with these great monsters a lot," I whispered. "Not much," Raphael said. *Something I said must have been funny because Freddie laughed a bit as we made our way outside*, Raphael whispered to himself. "So, how far is this lake?" I asked again. "It will be far from here if I remember from the old days," Raphael said. "Old days?" I questioned with an odd look on my face. "Yes, since the war against evil that happened back when your world was still young," Raphael explained. Raphael was still on the lookout for this human named *Murphy* that I told him about. *From the sounds of it, he must be an odd human that rules somewhere to still be alive*, the angel wondered.

I still don't think he gets that *Murphy* is a law and not something you can see. That's okay, I guess, but I'm going to tell him about it if we get a chance. Raphael moved quickly to the lake, and I followed,

I didn't know what to think about Behemoth, but it would be nice if he was as big as Ziz. We moved from tree to tree, almost like we were doing three to five-second rushes back at Bragg. Then, Raphael stopped suddenly, and I did the same. "What happened? We were doing so well," I whispered. Raphael turned slowly back at me. "A sunflower," Raphael whispered back. "Wait…what?!" I stuttered. I looked past him and saw a giant flower that was nothing like the sunflower humans know. First off, this thing had a woman's face at the center of it, it looked like something you might see on Pokemon. The flower was about four feet wide where the front was and looked like a flower until you get to the ground. I see why Raphael stopped suddenly because looking at us was another set of eyes with a large mouth filled with sharp teeth. "Raphael, can we get around this thing?" I whispered. "I'm not sure, these things have been around since the beginning. They have a good six-foot reach," Raphael whispered back. "Great, will this thing let us go back?" I questioned. Raphael hadn't moved a muscle since we almost walked into this thing. I started to look around for something to help Raphael and saw a tree branch lying on the ground. Making sure that there was nothing around to bite my head off before moving over to pick it up. "Hang on, Raphael, and get ready to move," I whispered. He said nothing, only nodded as I got ready to toss the tree branch to the left. I could see the monster slowly picking itself up. I tossed the branch, and it popped out of the ground like a snake and bit down on the branch as Raphael, and I watched. It ate the branch and slowly put itself back in the ground. "Well played, Freddie," Raphael whispered. Once it returned back to the ground and its head was cover, we moved slowly around him. "Well, that was nice," I said. Raphael looked up to the sky and saw something he didn't like, and we hid next to a tree. "It seems Gadreel knows what we are planning," Raphael said, looking to the sky. I looked up to see something floating. "Fucking Murphy," I murmured. Raphael looked over at me. "So, this Murphy is working for them? Then I spit on Murphy, may you die slowly," Raphael said. I couldn't help but let out a small laugh catching myself quickly.

    Since we left the church, Raphael was really thinking that *Murphy* is working for Gadreel and that they are looking for us and know that we are in the forest somewhere. I stood next to Raphael. The hammer would be at the center of the lake, and the only way to get there would be on Behemoth. "We better hope that this Behemoth can move fast," I said. Raphael said nothing to it, I know that it would be hard to get past them. So we ran from tree to tree, only stopping when something passed by overhead. "How much further is it to the water's edge?" I asked. "Not sure. I know one thing we must be getting close to. The number of trees is starting to thin out," Raphael answered. "Great, the only thing keeping us out of trouble is the fog, and we can't count on that for too much longer," he added. "Then we better find this Behemoth now, so we know where we're going," I said. Raphael looked up to the sky and smile. "Behemoth is close, come this way," he said, pointing into the fog.

I'm not sure what Raphael was looking at, but as long as he knew where he was going, I was okay with it. I looked up to see something moving in the clouds. "Damn, it's one of those fallen!" I snapped. Raphael looked up and turned at me. "No, that's Behemoth, my friend," Raphael said. It was like some kind of monster that I never saw before. This thing wasn't like Ziz and was a giant bird. This thing looked like an ancient mammal. I know why they called this thing Behemoth, it was big. As we got closer, I could see that he was just standing there at the lake's edge, his foot was the only thing I could see thru the fog. "Damn, everything in hell has to be huge or goddamn big," I said. "Come, we must be quick before we are spotted," Raphael said. He grabbed hold of my waist and jump thru the air, landing on his back. "So, how do we get him moving?" I questioned. Suddenly Behemoth moved, and I could hear thunder that was coming from below. "I think he's moving," I said, trying to keep my balance. Raphael stood firm as I was trying to stand on my feet, but I fell on my ass with every footstep. "I'm glad that we could find a boat to take us across," I said, falling again. "It would take us four months to get to the island on a boat," Raphael said. "Good then, I glad we got on Behemoth," I said, falling on my face again.

I had some trouble standing. Every time I would try to stand, I would fall. It led Raphael to wonder if the Creator should have given us a tail, but that would make us look weird. Behemoth was moving across the water slowly, and Raphael hoped to make it across before any of the Fallen saw us. I looked up, and before I fell, I pointed to the sky. "Incoming!" I shouted. Raphael looked up quickly to see a shadow landed on the back of Behemoth. "Hello, brother," the voice said. Raphael looked over to see a sister. A sister he hasn't seen in almost four hundred years. "Kasdaye, always good to see you," Raphael said using some of my sarcasm. "Well, so nice to get a warm welcome from my brother. I see you gained a sense of humor," Kasdaye smiled. Raphael stood there staring at her as I got to a knee behind her, trying my best not to be seen. "Where's the human, brother?" she asked. "What makes you think he is here?" Raphael questioned back. "Stop playing this game. I could call Gadreel here, and he would peel the truth from you," Kasdaye answered. If Gadreel will show up, it would be our end. I had managed to find a spot where I was just out of sight from Kasdaye. "I left the human in the forest so that I could be the hammer," I said. "You will show me where the human is, no tricks," Kasdaye said. Raphael could see the island come into view as the Behemoth walked along. Raphael needed to try and tell me to jump off, but anything he will do will make Kasdaye chase. Raphael looked past her to the spot where I was hiding. I looked up out of the space, and our eyes met.

    I had found a spot like a dip that this Kasdaye couldn't see me. She was tall, a little taller than me, and had dark-colored hair to match the odd blue eyes of hers. I looked over to Raphael, who looked at me before looking at his left. I looked that way, poking my head out a little, and saw an island in the fog. "Oh, I see now, nice, Raphael, my friend," I breathed. I look over to Raphael, who walked over to Kasdaye. "Listen, that human is the future of everything. If you kill him there will be nothing," Raphael murmured. I knew that was my cue, and I slowly got up and walked over to the edge. I looked over to see a long way down. "Shit, this sucks," I whispered to myself. "I don't care about that. I want the human!" Kasdaye snapped. I walked off the edge and into the lake below, hitting like a bag of rocks.

    Good, I managed to escape. I'm glad that Kasdaye is so single-minded, rare for an angel. "This way then," Raphael said, floating off into the air. Raphael will have to deal with her before she knows that I am long gone from her. Raphael flew through the air, followed closely by Kasdaye. He was trying to come up with a good plan for killing her without them knowing about it. From the sky, Raphael could see the lakeside through the fog. "He will meet me here once he got done talking with Mammon," Raphael explained. Kasdaye landed next to Raphael. "Call the human," Kasdaye sneered. "As you wish. Human, it's I, Raphael. You can come out," Raphael stuttered. Raphael hoped for his own sake he could pull it off. Otherwise, he will be in big trouble. They stood there for a while. Raphael could tell that Kasdaye was getting annoyed. Finally, she came up to my right. "Raphael, you better bring that human out, right now!" she snapped. Now came the ugly business. Raphael's knife came out slowly from his side, and he waited until she took one more step before he buried the knife deep into her back. She turned at Raphael slowly hitting him in the face as she fell to the ground. "Ra…pha…el," she stuttered. Raphael looked at her as the life slowly poured out onto the ground. "I must get back to Freddie," he said, looking up to the sky. Raphael looked up to see Gadreel floating, watching him from the clouds.

Hammer of the Damned

I stood on the lake edge doing my "best-wet dog impersonation" as I looked back to see fog and not much else. *I hope Raphael is okay*, I thought, walking over to a tree. I looked up to make sure that no one was coming before I headed into the woods. I could see a building not too far away. I could tell if anyone was around, so I darted from tree to tree. Finally, I poked my head out from the tree to see something walking around the building that looked just like the one I met Mammon in. "Great! I wasn't informed I was going to run into a welcome party," I whispered to myself. From the tree, I could see that she was a fallen just by the way she was dressed, just like that Kasdaye woman. From my spot, she looked like a five-dollar hoe and a twenty-dollar bitch. I had to go through the back if I wanted to keep them from finding me. I looked up to the sky, waiting for Raphael to come down and blast this white-haired hoe to last Friday. "I think Raphael might be in trouble," I whispered.

"Brother, it's always good to see you," Gadreel said, floating down to Raphael. "Good to see you too, brother," Raphael answered back with a bit of human sarcasm. "I'm guessing you're here with the human. Where is he?" Gadreel asked. "I lost him in this fog," Raphael said. "Look at what you did to sister. You should be saddened by this brother," Gadreel smiled. "My only sadness is that it wasn't you, brother," Raphael smiled back at him. Gadreel laughed like an animal. "I will ask you again, where is the human?" Gadreel questioned but Raphael said nothing. "You know what, brother, you could've had it all. The power, but you chose to listen to the Creator. The same Creator made those human monkeys and told us that we have to love them," Gadreel said. From the fog came another Fallen. "Azazel," Raphael murmured. Azazel said nothing, only taking his place next to Gadreel. "I see we have a bit of a family reunion here," Gadreel said. Azazel and Raphael were created at the same time as Gabriel and Jophiel. Azazel took a step forward, but before Raphael knew what will happen, Azazel had knocked Raphael into a tree a few feet back. Azazel picked Raphael up before pinning him against the tree. "So, will you talk with me, brother? Will you tell me where the human is?" he questioned. "Like I told your sister, I lost the human in the fog," Raphael insisted. "So tell me, how is Brother Gabriel? It must have been a close call for him, if it wasn't for that human, they do have their moments of strength," Gadreel said. "Why brother, does that make you feel bad, or is it the human. The human proofed you wrong," Raphael stuttered. "We will see how he does once I do away with you," Gadreel laughed as he pulled his sword out. Well, it looked like it is the end of Raphael when a loud horn sound filled the air. "Impossible!" Azazel said.

 I had moved behind the small building and spotted a wooden door that was falling off the hinges. "I hope they do take a collection, otherwise, I would tell these people to get their money back," I breathed. I moved the door and stepped inside, it was moldy and smelled like something died. "Okay, hammer, where the hell are you?" I said to myself. I looked around and tried not to make too much noise. I looked to the center of the room and saw something lying on top of a tomb-like grave. "This must be it," I breathed, looking around. There was something written on the side of the stone, "Evil will not stand, but good will not grow without it," I read. I wondered what the hell that meant as I stood up, a sound from the front door made me hide behind the tomb. I poked my head out to see nothing, and the front door was still closed. "Come on, Freddie, PTSD is fucking your day up right now," I whispered, trying to find a way to open the tomb. Suddenly the roof was destroyed, as wood and stone from the roof fell to the ground. "What the fuck?!" I shouted, hugging my body as close as I could to the tomb. From the sky came this long white hair woman that was sitting in the front of the building. "I knew I smelled a human, so you must be the one brother

Gabriel was trying to get out of here," the woman said. She had a dirty appearance as she landed and was wearing a black fish shirt that showed everything. "I guess you angel people don't believe in showers or wearing bras," I murmured. She laughed at it. "You're a funny man. Once I take you back to Gadreel, I will be the one that will get to kill you slowly," she said. "Who are you?" I like to know the name of the woman who is about to kill me, I guess. "I guess I could do that, I'm Penemue, sister of Kasdaye and Michael. And what is your name, human?" she asked. "Freddie," I frowned. "Good, I will put that on your gravestone later!" Penemue snapped. She pointed her finger at me, and a light shot out, barely missing me by the seat of my pants. The tomb behind me exploded into a hail of small rocks that covered me. "I see, so it's true...you have gained some power while you were with Gabriel," Penemue said. I looked up to her as she walked over. "I need something," I coughed. My hand came to rest on a handle, and I looked down to see a sledgehammer, but it wasn't just any sledgehammer. The thing was silver and had a black handle with some kind of weird writing on it. Penemue looked over at me as if I had slapped her monkey. "Impossible," she said. "Yeah, I've heard that word a lot lately. Doesn't do any justice for this," I smiled. "You fool, you have no idea what you have in your hands!" she shouted. "Yeah, Hammer of the Damned," I said. "You have the weapon of Malak, the Word of the Creator," Penemue said. "Thank you for telling me," I smirked. She fired another beam from her finger, and it hit the hammer, causing it to glow gold. "What are you doing?!" she screamed. "Lady, if I knew, I'm sure as hell wouldn't tell you anything," I said. Soon, the gold glowed. "Great, now what?" I stuttered. Suddenly the building I was in turned black, so dark I couldn't see a damn thing.

They led Raphael to the church, pushing him along until they came to the doors, and suddenly Azazel turned around. "Gadreel, something is going on over there," he said. Gadreel turned around and saw the same thing they all saw, a golden light that filled the air and shot out of hell to heaven. "Impossible!" Gadreel coughed. *Good, Freddie found the hammer, he still might have a chance at getting out of here*, Raphael thought. *I could tell that this wasn't part of their grand plan*, he added. "Seems like the human has proved his worth," Raphael breathed. "Shut up!" Gadreel snapped, slapping me in the face.

I felt like I was in space, I could feel a presence with me all around the darkness, but it wasn't evil, more like…a father, or some kind of higher power that was there with me. I could hear a voice like grandfathers talking about his old days. "So, you are Freddie Johnson, you continue to surprise me, human," the voice said. "Who are you?" I asked. "I am whom you humans called God, my child," the voice said. I think that was the point I spaced out of my brain had a long fart, I'm not sure though. "Sir…ahm…uh…Oh! Crap," I stuttered. If I knew I would have a sit down with the Lord. I would have put on my Sunday's best. "My son, you may ask me anything you wish," God said. Great, I had a lot of questions, but I only care about one. What's this person called the *Redeemer?*" I asked. "Something I made for the humans when I lost faith in you all the first time I sent the Great Flood. I wanted to make sure that in the end, you all will do the one thing that you all forgot," God said. I sensed that he was sad about this, that we, as His people forgot something. "What did we forget, sir?" I questioned. "You forgot how to love yourselves and the others. You use this *Science* just for you to love the real you. I want you to love your true self and your fellow brothers and sisters," He said. "Will this *Redeemer*, I mean me help them love again?" I asked. "Are you sure that you are the *Redeemer?* Maybe it was something that dies long ago, or you're really not the one," God answered. I smiled at this, hoping it wasn't true either. "Are you hoping that I have the answers for you, my child?" God asked. I was so surprised, the man upstairs was asking me a question. "I guess I want an answer," I answered. "If you are the *Redeemer*, then this whole journey for you will change. You will have to face true fear and master it as anyone has that wanted answers in life," God said. "My time with you grows short. I will leave you with this, hope is something you humans always have, but you never use it the way it should have been used. Use it, you're better than anyone, and you will have your answers," God said. I felt a light behind me and turned to see the hammer floating over to me. I took hold of it, and the golden light started to fade. The black around me changed and started to take shape, and soon I was back in the building with the Fallen, but she wasn't moving. "I'm getting the hell out of here before she starts back up again," I breathed and ran to the door. I hit it like a crazy man and knocked part of the door off the hinges. I heard a scream as the front of the building exploded, sending stone and small pieces of glass into the air. The force of the explosion sent me to the ground as Penemue flew through to air. "Shit!" I breathed.

Gadreel was watching the whole thing and saw the large black dome appear over the island. "What is that human monkey up to?!" he shouted. Raphael was watching as well, only hoping that Gadreel asked the right questions. It was rare for the Creator to talk to a human, but He did it a few times in human history. "Azazel, go over there and bring me that human!" Gadreel shouted. Raphael looked over to the tall Fallen as he took off into the air. "We both know what just happened. The Creator spoke to the human. The Creator will tell the man everything!" Raphael shouted. Gadreel looked over at him but said nothing, Raphael saw a little worry in his eyes that he never had seen before. Suddenly the black dome disappeared, and a booming sound echoed around. Gadreel let out a scream that could have been heard on that tiny island. "Stay safe, Freddie," Raphael breathed.

Penemue tackled me but couldn't hold on, and we both fell to the ground. She hit a tree as I rolled to a stop, I got up and kept running. The fog had disappeared around the building but started to return. "Great, I don't even know how the hell I'm going to get off this island," I said. I looked around for Behemoth but couldn't see him. I kept running through the wood when the sound of a scream came but it was just faint. *I hate to be that guy*, I said to myself as I shot through the trees. I could see the lakeside, but I was just wasting energy with no way to get off the island. Then a plan came to me that I know could work if they were stupid enough to believe it. I stopped at the water's edge as another fallen flew through the air. I'll have to play the silly human card on this one. I saw Penemue float over the trees. "Look at this, a human," the male Fallen said. He looked like a punk rocker with chains all over his pants and shirt. "Looks like he's done running around," Penemue smiled. "We're going to take you to Gadreel so he can feed on your bones, human," he said. I said nothing as Penemue took the hammer from my back. "You won't need this," she said. The male Fallen grabbed hold of my neck and floated up into the air with Penemue behind him, heading back to the Gadreel fucker that I should have killed.

Gadreel had said every word he could think of as he watched the island, making sure that I was brought to him. Finally, two black dots shot out from the island into the air. "Well, good news, I hope," Gadreel said, wearing a smile on his face. His brother and sister returned with me in tow. "We meet again, Freddie," Gadreel smirked. Raphael could tell that Gadreel had some unfinished business with me. "You again, I thought you died," Freddie said. Raphael looked over at me and saw that I was having some kind of trouble with my eyes. I kept blinking at him. *It must be a human thing*, Raphael thought. "What did the Creator say to you?" Gadreel asked. "He told me only what is needed to be known," I answered. "That sounds about right, but be specific" Gadreel questioned again. "That there was a great power in there," I said, pointing to the church. Raphael looked over at me with a slight smile on his face. "Well, this great power will be mine, human," Gadreel said. Azazel grabbed Raphael, and their sister grabbed me and took us to the church.

Good, just like I hoped. They're as stupid and stuck on themselves as I think. Gadreel opened the door and pushed Raphael inside, and I followed behind. "Where is this great power?" Gadreel questioned. I pointed to the upside-down cross at the center of the room. "Should we kill the human now?" Penemue asked. Gadreel smiled. "In time, sister. I want him to see me first destroy this great power," Gadreel said, walking over to the cross. "You're going to need the hammer," I said. Gadreel looked over to Penemue. "Give me that," he said, pointing to Penemue's waist. She tossed him the hammer, and he turned back to the cross. "Wait, there's something not right about this," Azazel stuttered. "Oh, would you like to destroy the power yourself instead, brother?" he questioned. "No, there's really something wrong here," Azazel insisted. "They have nothing left, we already have them. If they will try anything, we will destroy them," Gadreel said, floating into the air. "Penemue, make the human tell me how to make the power mine," Gadreel added. Penemue held me by my left arm. "Talk, human. Tell my brother how to make the power his," she said. "Okay, lady, take it easy. He must break those chains," I said. Gadreel slammed the hammer into the chains, breaking them. "Well, you have the great power, the great power of Mammon," I muttered. That's when Gadreel's eyes grew two sizes as a blast came out of the hole, hitting him and blinding the rest of us. *Damn it!* I heard a voice said as Mammon rose from the hole freed from his chains. He looked down to the group and pointed. "You humans are a man of your word. You freed me and brought me Azazel. I'm starting to like you, human," he boom dropping to the ground. The shockwave from his landing made the fog disappear. "Now for you, Azazel…" Mammon said. Before he finished, Mammon ran at him and hit him square in the chest, sending him to the sky. Raphael, now free, rose into the air and hit Gadreel with something that looked like lightning. "You make good plans, Freddie," Raphael said. "We need that hammer," I muttered. I looked around and saw it next to the hole. "I'm going for it," I said. Around me were fallen angels trying to stop a very pissed-off demon that was out for blood. Good luck with all that. "We need to get out of here!" Raphael shouted. "Make a run for the door," Raphael added. We broke out in a run and were stopped just short of the door by Gadreel. "You fucking human!" he snapped. "You wanted great power, and you got it, friend," I said with a bit of a smile on my face. Before he could say another word, Mammon came into the picture and hit Gadreel. Knocking him into the wall. "Off with both of you, you are in my way," Mammon said. "Will leave you to your work then," I muttered as Raphael and I ran past him and out the door. The forest was now clear of the fog as we ran down the path.

Year 3: Cain & The Sword of Damascus

The forest was mostly quiet, with the only noise being the sound of our footsteps as we made our way on the path. "You think they will follow us?" I asked. Raphael looked back, making sure that nothing was going to jump out at us. "I couldn't tell you. With any luck, Mammon has killed at least one of them, that would make the trip easier, and we wouldn't have to worry," Raphael answered. "I'm glad you came up with that speedy plan of yours," Raphael added. "Jophiel told me to stay on my feet and never drop my guard," I said. "Then I think Jophiel was a good teacher for you, Freddie," Raphael said. Finally, we came to a fork on the road. "So, is it left or right?" I asked. "Both ways will take us where we have to go. It's just that one way is harder than the other," Raphael answered. Right then and there, I didn't like the way he said it, it sounded like *Murphy* was about to raise his ugly head and say hello. "The path to the right will take us to the Mountain of Fools. The left will take us past the home of Cain, and from what I heard, he's not a nice man," Raphael said. You mean Cain, like the *Cain* that killed his brother Abel?" I questioned. "Yes, that guy," Raphael answered. "So, is he a demon or monster or something worst?" I questioned. "No, just a man, but when you're the first man to kill another, there is only one place for you," Raphael answered. "Then we go right, right?" I muttered. "Good choice, Freddie," Raphael smiled.

Gadreel was angry. He had gotten outsmarted by a human, and to make matters worse, they were chased by the demon Mammon. Gadreel sat alone thinking as Nimrod walked over to Azazel. "I take it, it didn't go well," Nimrod whispered. "No, but do not let Gadreel overhear you. Otherwise, you will be the king of fools," Azazel whispered back. "Kind of hard to move fast when you have an army of giants that want to eat everything they see," Nimrod said. Azazel smiled at it. "It might be a good thing that this happened because now we know that we must not take the human lightly next time," Azazel whispered. "What do you mean by that?" Nimrod asked. "I'm going to handle this myself, and I will bring the human back," Azazel said, walking away from Nimrod.

Freddie was an intelligent human, and it was his plan that saved our lives, Raphael thought. He thought that I, as a human, is more than just another human. Could he dare say that I could be the *Redeemer?* He learned two things in his time watching humans and one of them is that we are not to be laughed at. "We'll have to stop here. My time with you has ended," Raphael said. "Are you leaving, Raphael?" I asked. "Yes, but my little brother knows a little more about humans than I do," he said. Just as Raphael said that fire suddenly appeared in front of us, and out his brother Chamuel. "You two are late, what happened?" he asked. "Nothing big just got side-tracked by some fellow brothers and one sister," Raphael answered. "Let me guess. Gadreel?" Chamuel answered. "Yes, but he should have his hands full with demons right now, so you should have a safe trip," Raphael said. "I wouldn't say that it will be all that safe," I said. "I hope you're holding up well, Freddie?" Chamuel asked. "Oh, you know the usual running away from the demon, pissing off fallen angels, and riding giant monster around hell. I would have to pay money in the real world for this," I smiled. Chamuel looked over at Raphael and he started to laugh at it. "Raphael, has Freddie lost his mind?" Chamuel asked. "No, it's human sarcasm, brother. They use it when they are worried, from what I could tell," Raphael answered. I gave a smile as Chamuel looked back at me again with a puzzled look on his face. I still stood on the path as Chamuel went to join me. "Tell Jophiel I said hello," I said as we walked off.

Chamuel, from the look of his face, didn't know what a joke was and seemed worried about me losing my mind. If I lost it, I didn't know myself, but I do know one thing, we got Fallen after us, and I, for one, would like to get going. "Is Cain really a bad guy?" I asked, looking over at Chamuel. "No, but he was the first human to enter hell, so he has a special place here," Chamuel answered. From the sound of it, he might be some trouble, better stay on his good side if we meet him. The forest opened up to a wide-open area about a hundred feet wide with nothing overhead but the light from whatever is up there. "I always wanted to ask, where does the light in the sky come from if we're in hell?" I asked. "From heaven, but the deeper into hell we go, the darker it will be. Once we get to Sheol, it will be cold as well as dark," Chamuel said. I looked up into the sky. "I wonder if my grandma is up there watching," I muttered. We walked along the path until we came back under the trees as something caught my eye. "Did you see that?" I said, looking for something that I thought was a person. Chamuel looked around as well. "We are being watched by someone," he said. I pulled out the hammer. "Let them try someone, and I'll knock their block off," I said, holding up the hammer. Chamuel looked at it and then back out into the trees. Questions filled my head, could it be Cain or Gadreel returning to try to kill me again? I will say this for Gadreel, he doesn't know how to quit, he would make a good army guy if he wasn't a terrible angel ready to cut my head off. I put the hammer back on my belt and started to walk. After a while of walking, we came to the edge of a small lake. With a house on a small piece of land out in the middle. "Who lives out there?" I asked. "Cain," Chamuel muttered. "Well, this is a surprise," a voice said from behind us. We both turned to see a man standing wearing a brown jacket and jeans, holding a box in his hands. "Always good to see you Chamuel, what brings you out here in hell?" the man added. "Cain, I see you mellowed in your years," Chamuel said. Oddly both Cain and Chamuel hugged like two old friends that haven't seen each other in a while. "Wait, you are Cain, right?" I asked. Cain looked over at me, "Yes, what were you expecting, I am covered in blood or something" Cain smiled, holding out his hand. I shook it and felt the strength that was in his hands. He could have broken my hand if it wasn't for the powers I had. "Come, I have some tea ready," Cain said. He led the way walking along the lake edge until we came to a boat. "A boat," I murmured. "Yeah, unless you want to swim?" Cain smiled. "I like him, he's funny," I whispered to Chamuel.

We started rowing across the lake, starting with me and Cain rowing. "I see they keep you guys in shape where you're from," Cain said. "I try. When I don't eat pie and sleep, I might do a little something," I said. "I like him, Chamuel. He's funny," Cain said. Chamuel was watching Cain and me closely, not saying a word the whole time to the island.

Chamuel found it odd that the two humans got along so quickly. He thought for sure that we would hate each other, but it is a surprise. The boat came to a stop on the island's edge, and Cain stepped off the ship first. Chamuel and I followed as Cain opened his door and saw a room covered in mostly sunflower. "Wow, you love you some flowers," I muttered. "No, not really. I use the oil from them for heating my lamp," Cain said pointed to his left. There is this corner where his bed and a small desk at. "How do you live in hell? So far, everything or everyone I've met either wants to eat me or kill me," I said. "It's really not that hard, young one, just stay out of everyone's way," Cain explained. I said nothing to it, Chamuel thought he was thinking of the same thing. Cain walked over to his stove and brought over a pot of tea, and cups that were made of wood with a lite finish. "I see you still do woodwork" Chamuel smiled. Cain looked over at Chamuel. "Yes, but my brother was better at it than I was," Cain laughed. I said nothing, and there was a long silence in the air that hanged there for some time. Cain sat down and looked over at us. "Ask me, young one," Cain muttered. I had a look of shock on my face that I couldn't hide. "Ask you what, sir…?" I murmured. "About my brother, I can hear that question rolling around in your head since you first met me," Cain said. I, who was sipping my tea, put the cup down and looked over at Chamuel. "Cain has the power to read people's minds, given to him by one of the Princes of Hell," Chamuel explained. "Wow, that's cool. Okay! Uhm, why did you kill your brother?" I asked. Cain looked away from me. "I was young, and maybe angry, but mostly I was young," Cain answered. "I hate to pry, but I can tell what happened to you in the sand long ago. The death of that woman wasn't your fault," Cain added. I looked over to Cain. "I know, but I still think I could do more," I muttered. Chamuel saw a tear rolling down my face. "Cain, we need your help to find the way out of here. Can you help us?" Chamuel asked. Cain stood up and walked over to the small window. "If you leave here and walk on the path, you go like you're going to the snow-covered caps. You will leave the forest and walk into Sheol," Cain answered. "Wait, you said if we leave here?" Freddie muttered. "Yes, Azazel is headed this way. You have some time until he gets here, but if he finds you here, he will kill you," Cain said. Chamuel stood up and walked over to the door. "Freddie, it's time to go!" Chamuel snapped. He opened the door and headed out to the edge of the island, and I followed. "I guess it's a good thing he can read minds," I said. I helped Chamuel push the boat into the water, Chamuel and I rowed like our lives depended on it because it's very well might have. "Great! I take it that Azazel is pissed after what Raphael and I did to him," I said. "True, but I think he has different orders than what Gadreel is telling him to do!" Chamuel shouted as the boat hit the other side. We both hopped out and started running as fast as we could through the forest. Chamuel heard the sound of thunder fill the sky. "Oh no! He's close," Chamuel muttered. I looked back and fell, hitting the ground hard. "Fuck!" I shouted. Chamuel turned around to pick me up, and he saw my eyes grew wide in a look of terror, Chamuel turned to see Azazel behind with his blade out and a sick smile on his face.

Azazel appeared out of nowhere and had got behind Chamuel and cut him across his stomach. Chamuel tried to hold his inside in, but then came Azazel stabbing Chamuel in the side of the head. I stood up and hit Azazel with all the power and anger I had and knocked him into a tree. "Chamuel," I said, going to his side. Chamuel's eyes were dead, and anything he had to say would die with him. I looked over to Azazel whose eyes met mine, so I stood up. "What do you want on your tombstone?" I asked.

Cain had poured out the rest of the tea when a voice came to him. "Cain, Cain, can you hear me?" the voice asked. "It's always good to hear from you, Jophiel," Cain answered. "Did Chamuel and Freddie come to see you?" Jophiel questioned. "Yes, but they left in a hurry. Azazel was after them, so they left," Cain answered. "I lost contact with Chamuel, I fear the worst," Jophiel muttered. "Is that man the *Redeemer*?" Cain asked. "Yes, at least Michael thinks so," Jophiel answered. "Then Azazel might kill them both," Cain said, walking to the door. "I was going to ask you for help," Jophiel murmured. "I know, and I'm heading out now," Cain said. "Thank you," Jophiel said. "I think this will be the last talk we'll have, old friend," Cain said, walking out the door. He stepped out to the sounds of trees been knocked down and saw one tree fell. "If they will be close to the Sword of Damascus, then he might have a chance to stop him once and for all," Cain said, running to the back of the house. He grabbed the extra boat and pulled it to the front, and hopped in, rowing as fast as he could to the other side and pushed it into the water.

My fight with Azazel mainly was one-sided, as if he was letting me hit him. After knocking him into a tree, I stopped and stayed right where I was as he pulled himself up. "Why not come at me, human?" he questioned. "Born at night wasn't last night!" I shouted. Azazel stood up, and I saw why he was known as the Angel of the Dead. He wore all black and was taller than any angel I've seen so far. "You are wise, but that won't help you with me, human," Azazel muttered. I had two feelings at that point, one, business was about to pick up, and two, a sword appeared in his left hand. I pulled out the hammer that was resting on my back and stepped forward. "That won't help you, that hammer will only work on damned souls and I am not one of them," he said. "Still, I'm sure if I hit you with this, it will still hurt," I muttered. "That's the problem. If you…hit me," Azazel smiled. I knew that smile from a lot of people that knew something you didn't. Even in Afghanistan, when they look at you and smile, they always know something you didn't. I watched as his body started to turn black and slowly sink into the ground. I watched until he disappeared. "Great," I breathed. *He's going to attack below me, maybe,* I thought, but the answer came in the form of something hitting me in the chest. "Now you see why I let you hit me earlier, now you will die human," Azazel said. I took a step back, and something hit me in the back before tossing me into the air. I hit the ground with a cloud of dust. "What is this? No human could survive a hit from my sword," he said. The dust came up around me, and for a moment, it took shape, as something metal hit me in the face. I smiled. *This guy made himself invisible, I could use it, but I need more dust or sand,* I thought. "Why can't I kill you, human?!" he shouted and knocked me to the ground. *Just like the other Fallen, he gets angry very easily,* I thought. *Now I had to find a way to make him visible because I might be running out of time.*

Jophiel sat under his tree to the left of his house, he was soon joined by Michael packing his bag. "It's just as I feared, Chamuel is dead, and

Freddie is all by himself," Jophiel muttered. "I'm going to him," Michael said. "Wait, Cain is headed to Freddie as well. We need to stay true to the boy if he is indeed the *Redeemer*, then he will make a way," Jophiel said. "But what about Chamuel?!" Michael snapped. "I know he's your little brother, but we must wait. This human doesn't need a babysitter," Jophiel smiled. Michael looked away from him as Jophiel looked up to the sky. "Freddie is somebody here," Jophiel muttered.

I was running through the forest, being chased by Azazel but unable to see him. "Are you scared, human? You should be. Fear your death," Azazel laughed. The forest opened up to an opened field burned by something at the center of the scorched earth. It was a green piece of ground with a sword sticking out from it. I didn't think about what the sword was doing at the center of a great burnt donut, but I ran to it like it was calling my name. Just as I touched it, the ground around me caught fire, I heard a scream cut through the air. I saw a body flying into the air burning as it did. "What the hell is this?" I said to myself. "That is the Sword of Damascus," a voice shouted. I looked through the fire to see Cain standing there. "Can you turn this off, friend" he called. "Azazel killed him!" I shouted back. "I know, that's why I'm here!" he shouted back as the fire started to die down. Cain walked over to me. The smoke was thick, like smoking a pig for dinner. "Jophiel said that you might need some help. I will help you get to where you need to go," Cain smiled. "Thanks, I hope he doesn't come back," I muttered. Cain helped me to my feet. "So, does this sword have a story to tell?" I asked. "Yes, everything in hell will tell you a story. If you listen well enough, you can hear it," Cain answered. We walked back into the forest and past a fallen log. We saw a dead body of some sitting up against the wall. "You said that this sword has a story, do you know it?" I asked. "If I am not mistaken, I think you're holding the sword of one of the Four Horsemen," Cain answered. "You mean the Four Horsemen?" I trailed off. "Yes," Cain said with a puzzled look on his face. "Why? I mean, is there more than one group calling themselves the Four Horsemen?" Cain questioned back. "You could say that," I said. Cain said nothing to it as we started to pass more dead bodies. "I hate to meet the thing that did this to them," I whispered. "Something killed these Nephilim," Cain said, looking down at the bones. From what I could see it looked like something was chewing on its bones. "But what could kill a Nephilim? I thought those things were like the Pitbulls of this place," I said. "This was done by a sword, an angelic sword…it's Azazel," Cain said. "Wait, you mean, the guy that flew out of here did this?!" I spoke with amazement. "He was a monster not too long ago. He killed and ate these Nephilim all the time," Cain said. "Great, an angel that likes mass murder, what's next?" I questioned.

Azazel, the Angel of Death

Azazel crashed to the ground, still on fire, after rolling around, he was now looking up at the black sky. "Stopped by a human, impossible," he murmured. He got to his feet and cursed the sky before turning to his left. "The human will die, and all his hope will go with him," Azazel said, taking off his cloak. He tossed it to the ground, and still up, burns covered most of his body.

Cain was moving fast through the forest, at first, I was surprised by this, but then I remember that he lived in the forest for a long time. It was just something that he did every day. "So will this Azazel guy leave us alone now that he got burned by this sword?" I asked. Cain looked back at me, stopping in mid-step. "No, you just made him mad as hell, and that is one angel you don't want to piss off," Cain answered. "Great, wish I knew that before I burned the guy," I said. Cain smiled. "You are one hell of a human, Freddie," he said. "I try when I'm not being chased by fallen angels," I smiled back. Cain turned and started walking again. "So this Azazel guy is the Angel of Death, how did he draw the short end of the straw?" I asked, walking beside Cain. "I don't know the full story, it happened after the Great Fall," Cain said. "Let's say for this case that I don't know what that is," I whispered. "I heard this from one of the Fallens that use to live in this forest. Long ago, when the Creator cast out Lucifer, there was one fallen angel that still wanted to do his job," Cain said. "I'm guessing that was Azazel," I muttered. Cain said nothing but nodded yes as he spoke. "Because he had fallen, he couldn't have a job, the Creator took that job from him, so he found an angel and took his sword as his own. The real Angel of Death was named Samuel, and once his weapon was taken, he became one of you," Cain said. "Wait, he became human? That's shitty," I said. "Wait, that means that he's dead now, right?" I asked. "No, the Creator only gave him an everlasting life," Cain answered. "Cool, so he can basically live forever. Not a bad trade, but, can he get his weapon back?" I questioned. "Yes, if someone kills Azazel, his sword will return to the rightful owner," Cain answered. By this time, we had walked into a large group of dead Nephilim lying around. "He killed all these poor creatures?" I said. "Yes, once Azazel got the powers from Samuel, he needed someone to test it on," Cain said. "One-second thought, I hope I get to see him again," I muttered. Cain looked over at me. "So I can kill him," I added.

Gadreel stood at the foot of a great mountain as Nimrod walked over to him. "Sorry to tell you this, but Azazel went after the human," Nimrod said. "I know Nimrod, I've known for some time now," Gadreel said. Nimrod said nothing to it. "Azazel is nothing like the other angels, he's a damn animal, and good at it" Gadreel smiled. "So, do you want me to go help him?" Nimrod asked. "No, you will only get in his way. We'll go to Gehenna and wait for the human," Gadreel answered. "Gehenna?" Nimrod said, puzzled. "He's going to see his daddy, and I want to be there to kill the human with his father watching," Gadreel smiled.

Cain and I stepped out into a large field in the distance were a huge snow-covered mountain. "What is that?" I asked, pointing to the mountain. "That is the Mountain of Daystar, but I'm not so sure what's in there," Cain answered. I said nothing looking off at the mountain, Cain turned and walked to the left, following a path. "Aren't we going to cut through the field?" I asked. "No, that's not a field, it's a massive ocean," Cain answered, tossing a small stone into the field. The stone hit with a splash, and the water rippled out. "Oh wow...." I muttered. "We must ride Leviathan to get over there," Cain said. "I would have walked right into the water like a dumbass," I whispered. "I like that about you, Freddie," Cain said. "What's that?" I asked. "You tell it like it is not too many people do that anymore," Cain answered. "I don't know about that, I'm just myself," I said. "What a wonder it must be," Cain muttered.

Cain looked back at me, I followed close behind him as we walked. "Jophiel, are you there? We're getting close to Leviathan," Cain said. "Good, Azazel will come and attack you there. That would be my best guess," Jophiel answered. "What about Freddie? So far, I have shown him everything he needed to see," Cain explained. "Good, once he makes it to Michael, he will do the rest," Jophiel said. "You know how much I don't like sending someone to their doom," Cain muttered. "I'm sorry about this, but the Creator's word is the law. We can't turn away from it now," Jophiel said. "You mean…." Cain trailed off. "Yes, the Creator is now watching. He wants the boy to go through a trial, if there was a way for him not to go through it, I would try, but…." Jophiel trailed off. "I know, the Creator must see everything," Cain said. Cain felt a hand touch his shoulder and turned to see me talking to him. "You okay, Cain, you went full robot on me," I said. "Sorry, just in deep thought, that is all," Cain explained. "Must be some deep thought," I murmured. "What were you saying?" Cain asked. "I was asking you what is in the Daystar Mountain," I answered. It stopped Cain in his tracks. "The Prince of Hell that has had a hand at everything. Has happened to you from the beginning," Cain explained. "Okay, that tells me a lot," I said. "I don't know much about that place, just what I heard, and what I have heard isn't good," Cain said. I asked nothing more about the place but turned now and then, watching it. Cain hoped that Michael will tell me everything, there is still a story for me to tell, and it's my story now.

Azazel peeled the burned flesh from his body as he watched us. "That bastard, that human monkey. I will make him pay for this," he stuttered to himself. Cain was now walking again after telling me something, now, we would need a ride to the other side of the Great Mirror Lake. Azazel's blue eyes burned with hate for me, and he couldn't wait until he had another shot at me. He stood up, peeling the last of the burns from his hand, and disappeared behind a tree, waiting until his time was right.

Cain was watching the water of the large lake closely, and he pointed out to the middle of the water. "There she is," Cain pointed. I followed his finger to a large head that was moving to the lake's edge. "I'll take a guess and say that's Leviathan," I said. Cain said nothing, only nodding as Leviathan came to a stop. "Cain, what are you doing here?" a voice boomed. "Good to see you too, Leviathan, I like you to meet a friend.

This is Freddie, Freddie, my friend Leviathan," Cain smiled. "That's one big girlfriend," I murmured. "What's a girlfriend?" Cain asked. I looked over at him and said nothing as we stepped on top of her head if I could call it. I wasn't going to look under the hood to find out. I could feel Leviathan turning in the water and watched as the lake edge got further away. "So, how far do we have to go?" I asked. "We will have to be on the water for one whole week," Cain answered. "Damn, should have brought a book on this trip," I whispered. "It's not too bad, we can talk. I hope you people talk to each other?" Cain asked. "No, we have something called Facebook and something called the phone," I answered. "A phone, a Facebook. I don't think I could live in that world of yours," Cain muttered. "You and me, friend," I laughed. Suddenly, something from the sky hit the ground with the force of an explosion. "Jesus, what the hell was that?!" I shouted. "Seems you will have your shot at Azazel again," Cain muttered. From the brown cloud stepped Azazel, this time, I was able to see him, and he was ugly. Most of his clothes were burned, and his blue eyes and pale skin showed through the burn holes. "I guess it was too much to ask that you died somewhere," I said. "No, human. I'll destroy you this time," he said. Leviathan looked over at us. "Azazel, you should be with your bastard brother and sister," Leviathan boomed. "You shut up, sea bitch, this is between this monkey and me," Azazel seethed. "Monkey? Damn, can't just be a human?" I whispered to Cain. "Azazel, you have no job here, no one has died!" Cain shouted. "Not yet, Cain, but soon, both of you will die," Azazel snapped. Cain and I said nothing waiting for an attack from Azazel as Leviathan spoke. "You know the rules, you can't use your power here unless someone is dead or you have been attacked". I looked over at Cain, "Is this true?" I questioned. "Yes, but I don't think that will help us out now," Cain whispered. "So this guy is still going to attack us," I said. "It will be a sure thing, Freddie, like the sunrise," Cain said. That's when Leviathan struck, dropping her head on top of Azazel. "Come both of you, I don't know how long that will keep him down," Leviathan said. "Nice shot," I said. Cain and I jumped on the head of Leviathan, and she went into the water as we were watching the spot where Azazel was now lying at. "He's going to wake up with a big headache and pissed at the world," I said. "Leviathan, take us to Baal," Cain shouted. "Are you sure about that? He's not the type to have a guess. He's still locked up, no thanks to Gadreel," Leviathan boomed. "No choice, we might be able to free him, maybe," Cain said. Leviathan said nothing, but I could feel that she changed direction. "So, who is this Baal?" I asked. "A Prince of Hell Azazel wouldn't dare go on to his island," Cain said. "Okay, Baal then, let's see what happens," I said.

Baal & Leviathan

The ride to Baal's island was long, but it was still a surprise when I saw the island come into view. The fog was covering it, so the only thing I could see was a castle. As we got closer, I noticed that it was made out of gold. "Damn! Must have money, hookers, and blow in there to last three lifetimes," I said. "What?!" Cain said with a puzzled look on his face. "Nothing, just an inside joke," I muttered. "I hope you're sure about this, you can still change your mind," Leviathan said. "Well, we can't turn back now, we're almost there," I said. Leviathan came up smoothly to the land, not making a sound. I wonder what it was like to live in a place like that as we hopped off Leviathan. "If you need me, Cain, give a whistle, and I'll come," Leviathan said as its head disappeared under the dark green water. "So, what are we going to do here?" I asked, looking over at Cain. "We're going to free Baal and hope that he won't kill us," Cain answered with a weak smile. "Fuck. That's some plan, I couldn't make a more crazed, half-baked plan if I had *Murphy* on speed dial," I muttered. "This doesn't sit well with me either, Freddie, but he's the only thing we got right now," Cain said. I said nothing to this as we walked into the low bush covered with some kind of black tar. "What the hell is this shit?" I snapped as I got stuck to a tree branch. "The Evil of Men now covers you, try not to get any on your mouth or eyes," Cain answered walked past me. "Why? Wait... maybe it's better if I don't ask a question," I said. Cain said nothing as

I followed closely behind him, as the castle covered in fog now waited like a lost pet waiting for its master.

Azazel pulled himself from the hole and shook the cobwebs out, and looked around. "That fucking human will pay for this with his blood," Azazel said. Azazel tried to fly but couldn't gain any air. "What? How?" he said, touching his wings. A pain shot through his back. "That sea bitch broke one of my wings," Azazel seethed. He stepped out of the hole and looked out into the water that looked like an open field. "That human has the devil's luck," Azazel grumbled. Azazel started to glow a light yellow that was blinding. "Now we will have our moment in the sun," Azazel muttered. As the light could be seen by any demon, and Nephilim around.

Gadreel was standing in an open field when a blinding yellow light filled the sky. "Well, that was sooner than I hoped," Gadreel muttered. "Come. Let us hope that he kept the human in one piece," Gadreel added as he floated into the air. He was followed by Asbeel and Penemue. "Move the Nephilims to Gehenna. Just in case the human makes it there," Gadreel said, flying off to the yellow light.

Moving through the forest was like playing the game Frogger, every few minutes, we would move, only to get stuck somewhere else and have to go back and find a new way. Or if that's not your game, I could play a mean game of Pitfall too. We walked out of the bushes. Well, I walked out, Cain kind of fell out rolling beside me. "Thank the Creator we are out of that mess," Cain said. The only real problem we had was that we were cover in the black tar mess. "I hope this guy has a washing machine," I said. Cain looked over at me. "Washing machine? What's that?" he asked. "Something that washes clothes," I answered. "You have something like that in your world?" Cain asked again. "Yes, walking around smelling like an ass isn't good for anyone," I answered. We walked up to the edge of a small river that cuts through the brimstone side and disappeared in the castle's base. "Wow, this place is bigger than I thought," I said. Cain crossed the brimstone and walked up to the side of the castle. "Now we need to find the door," Cain said. "Shouldn't be too hard with a big castle-like this," I smiled. "If you say so, friend. I never count eggs before they hatch," Cain smiled back, walking along. I followed, and after turning a corner, there was a large door that was closed up. "How the hell are we going to open this joker?!" I shouted. "If we could jump over the wall, we would be fine," Cain said. "I think I can help with that," I muttered. I took hold of Cain and jump. Well, more like a Superman jump to the top of the wall. I let go of Cain to see a look of pure shock on his face. "Yeah, I should have told you that I could do that," I muttered. "That could have been useful walking through the forest," Cain grumbled. "Yeah…if you want a tree branch stuck up your ass when I landed," I said, looking back at him. Cain looked away. "Okay, point well taken," he said. We looked over to the other side and saw a courtyard-looking thing below us. "I could drop us down there," I said. "No, we'll walk. If there is someone in here, whatever is down there knows you have some kind of power within you," Cain said. "Okay, then we better find some stairs," I said, looking out over the island. From up where we were, it wasn't too bad. I could see the whole island and the field-like water passed that until a bright light blinded me. "Maybe we should tell them to turn off the blinder," I whispered to Cain, covering my eyes. "That my young friend in trouble," Cain muttered. "What do you mean?" I asked. "Azazel. Azazel is calling for help," Cain answered. "Oh hell, not again," I muttered to myself. "We may need to hurry," Cain said, looking around. "Oh, okay," I said back. Cain started running for a door to our right, and I followed, hoping that we can free this Baal guy.

    We made our way down the stairs. I stayed close behind Cain as we came out in an empty courtyard. "So, now what?" I asked. Cain sensed that I didn't want to meet Azazel again, and I would be right. Azazel would have help with me this time, and nothing would stop them from killing both of us. "We need to free Baal. He's the only one that might have a shot at stopping them!" Cain shouted. I nodded as we looked around the courtyard, but the only thing we saw was four rows of dead trees and a dried-out pond to our right. "Where the hell is this guy?!" I asked. "He must be inside," Cain said, running for the large opening in front of us. The opening led us into the inside of the castle, and the gold's shine almost blinded us. Baal has some good taste, I thought as we stopped at the center of two choices, left or right. "This is like trying to find a needle in a haystack," I muttered. "Why would you want to try and find a needle in a haystack?" Cain asked. "Figure of speech, my friend," I answered. "Oh, I see," Cain said, still not getting what he was trying to say. We went left and ran to the end of the hallway and turned the corner to see the red light on the ceiling. "I'm guessing this is the way," I pointed. Cain put his hand on my shoulder. "Something or someone is here with us," Cain whispered. I said nothing, only looking forward like I was waiting for an attack to come. Stepping out from the dark red hallway was a tall woman, wearing all black with two blue orbs for eyes looking back at us. "What do you two want?" the woman asked. Cain stepped forward. "I'm here to talk with Baal. Can we speak with him?" Cain asked. "Baal is at the bottom of the castle, held against his will inside the mirror," the woman answered. "A mirror?" I asked. "Yes. Come, I will show you," the woman replied. We followed the woman to an old staircase in a large opening and a peculiar sight.

There was a large opening at the bottom of the stairs, it was lit by torches lined the wall. "We must be at the bottom of the castle," I said, looking over to Cain. The woman leading us was dressed in some kind of black cloud that followed her around. The eyes are what gave me the creeps, they were a cloudy blue that felt like they were looking into your very soul. I looked ahead to see a large mirror covering the whole wall, and from the look of it, they put it up in a hurry. The mirror was about twenty feet tall and almost sixty feet wide. "Damn. Talk about looking good," I muttered. A voice boomed suddenly from thin air. "What is it you want?" I stopped and looked over to Cain, who pointed to the mirror. I looked at it, and appearing in the mirror was a sizeable monster-like creature. It had three heads, but none of them were the same. In the center of the thing was a man's head, to the right of it was the head of a toad and to the left was a cat head looking down at us. All of it sat on large spider legs. "Whoever made this guy might need some kind of mental help," I said. By this time, all three heads looked over at us. "What do a human and the world's first murderer want from me?" the voice boomed. Cain stepped forward. "We need your help. There are forces after us that want to undo what we have started. We have a trip that we must finish," Cain said before Baal stopped him. "There is nothing I can do to help you, since Gadreel used this mirror on me, I have been trapped here for almost a hundred years," the monster explained. "Hello, sir. Can you tell us how we can help you to get out of there?" I asked. "Human, I would need divine intervention to free me from this mirror," Baal answered. It was hard talking to a thing with three heads, you don't know which head to face. "Well, what now?" I whispered. Cain looked at me before turning back to the mirror. "Does it have to be an angel, or could a Fallen free you too?" Cain asked. "It doesn't matter, but why would one of them come to help me?" he asked back. "We have four of them coming after us and we can trick at least one of them into freeing you," Cain explained. Baal said nothing for a few seconds before started talking. "Yes, but they would have to use their weapon and break the mirror themselves," he said. I looked over at Cain, who had a weak smile on his face. "I see one of us has a crazy half-ass plan," I said, slapping my hands together.

Azazel tried once more to fly, only to fall to the ground. He stood up as Gadreel floated down to him. "I see you ran into the human and a brother," Gadreel said. "Yes, the brother is gone, but the human still has help from the murderer," Azazel said. "Cain? Why would Cain help the human?" Gadreel muttered. "Where did they go?!" Gadreel snapped. Asbeel and Penemue landed behind him. "To the castle of Baal," Azazel said. Gadreel said nothing to this, only pointed to the sky, and Asbeel and Penemue took off. "Baal isn't the one I'm worried about, but the big demon is. Let's try again and kill them this time," Gadreel said, putting his arm around Azazel's waist and floated into the air.

I had a feeling that this plan of Cain's was a little crazy, but it was just maddest. We stood in the courtyard waiting for Azazel to come while he told me the rest of the plan. "You must have been born on Saturday," I muttered at him. The whole plan hoped that Azazel came with backup and followed us to the mirror, then hope that one of them wants to kill me with their arrows and would break the glass. Man, if I could live off of wishes and hope, then I would be rich. "Cain, we got company," I said. Cain looked over to the left and saw the same thing. Four fallen angels coming right at us. "Inside, now!" Cain shouted. I didn't need to be told twice, and I went back inside the castle. I heard what sounded like something hitting the ground behind us and footsteps. "Shit! They're coming!" Cain shouted, turning the corner. Something shot off the walls like a gunshot as we saw the mirror that we covered up before we left to come into its view. We entered the room. All the torches in the room almost went out as I stopped in front of the mirror. Waiting for something to get fired my way. I heard footsteps as something entered the room. "You are a good human, but not good enough," a voice said. Stepping into the light came Gadreel and his three other goons. "Not a bad plan, but not also good," I whispered to Cain. Cain said nothing as Gadreel stood less than two feet away. "Now I could only wonder what your plan could be," Gadreel said, clapping his hands. Azazel didn't waste any time and jumped at me, knocking me to the ground. "Enough Azazel, the human can't do anything now" Gadreel smiled. Azazel's breath smelled like a trash can, and he's seen better days. "Well, you asked me before why we have plan Bs. Well, this is why," I said. "Now!" I shouted. The woman appeared suddenly and shut the door before anyone could do anything. "What the hell was that?!" Asbeel said, looking over at Gadreel. I must say even Gadreel couldn't say anything to it. "What are you trying to do, human?" he asked. "We had the woman put something on the door that will keep all of us here until the world's end. I think that's what she said," I smiled. Asbeel walked over to the door and touched it and was hit with some kind of power. Gadreel was angry and grabbed hold of me by my neck. "You will undo your plan, human. Undo it, now," Gadreel seethed. "Sure, then. But you need to kill us," I choked. "Fine, human, you wish to plan that game," Gadreel said, dropping me to the ground. I could only wonder what the angel had in mind.

I was looking up and Gadreel walked over to the mirror. He pulled off the large cover that we found and took a step back. "See the mirror? It's a great weapon that was used by Daystar himself. Inside the mirror, time is nothing, the only thing you will know is emptiness," Gadreel said. "So, what?" I asked. "Well, human, I'm going to send you into the mirror, and you can join Baal and talk about nothing until the end of time!" Gadreel shouted. He put his hand up to the mirror, and it started to glow. "This isn't good," I muttered. A hole opened on the mirror, and before I knew it, I was sucked into it. Gadreel smiled as he walked over to the mirror. "I was hoping to eat you but I guess this would be better," Gadreel smiled. The mirror's glow slowly faded as Gadreel turned at Cain. "And as for you, first murderer, killer of men, I should get rid of you for giving me this type of trouble," Gadreel said, walking over to Cain. "Let me kill Cain and that sea bitch Leviathan!" Azazel snapped.

Gadreel looked over at Cain as if he was thinking about it. "I need him to get us out of here," Gadreel muttered. He turned back to the mirror. "I hope you like it in there, you're going to be there for a long time," Gadreel said, knocking on the mirror.

I was covered in darkness, and I couldn't see anything until a light floated over at me. "*Murphy*, you fat cocksucker," I breathed, looking around. "I see your plan didn't work," a voice said. I tried to find where the voice came from, but the only thing that I could see was a pair of red-colored lines. I walked over and soon saw that the red lines were really eyes, cat eyes. Baal was a lot bigger than Buer. He was as big as a six-story building. All three of the heads were probably looking at me. I could feel the eyes on me. "My plan is coming along," I said. "Getting trapped in this mirror is part of your plan too, human?" Baal asked. "Just a little setback, that's all. Cain will handle things on his end and he will be okay," I smiled. I couldn't tell if Baal was smiling or just not giving a shit anymore. "Looks like you will be stuck in here with me human for the rest of your life," Baal boomed. I looked around, but there was no point. I couldn't see anything, and even if I could get out of here, I still would have to deal with Gadreel. "How long have you been in this mirror?" I asked. "One hundred years, and maybe one hundred more," Baal answered. I could hear the loss in his voice and I thought to myself that a Prince of Hell just let it end like this. "Don't worry, Gadreel is stuck in that room, so he won't be able to come out," I said. "Human, that doesn't help us much," Baal said. His cat and toad head looked down at me as I looked out into the darkness. I couldn't see much past my face, and if there was a way out, I couldn't see one. "Can you tell me how they got you in the mirror?" I asked. The cat head looked away as now just the toad head was looking at me. "They came one day and wanted to trade me gold for the same mirror. I told them, no, but they kept asking until I said yes, in the end, they managed to trap me inside, and now I'm stuck, unable to get out. I turned out to the darkness," Baal explained. "This makes no sense, what if they got stuck in here too. They had to make a way out so that they couldn't get trapped either," I said. "We need an angel weapon, that is the only way out," Baal said. "Great, and we don't have one of those lying around this place," I muttered. Just then, from behind me, a light glowed. "Human, what is that on your back?" Baal questioned. "I don't know," I said, trying to grab at my back. The light was coming from the sword. "You should have told me your plan, human. Excellent," Baal smiled. I still didn't understand what was going on, but I rolled with it anyway. "Yeah, I almost forgot about this old girl," I laughed. "Now, you must try to get us out," Baal said, watching and waiting. Good, now how in the blue hell do I do that?

Cain watched as they tried to knock down the door with everything they had but still couldn't get free. Cain must tell me because I always have a plan. Even Gadreel was turning red already due to anger as Azazel's great power couldn't move the door. "This is impossible, how could we get trapped by a human? A fucking human!" Gadreel shouted, knocking over a table and turning it into five pieces that littered the stone floor. "Tell us, Cain, how do we free ourselves from this room?" Azazel asked. "You should ask the human, he is the only one that knows," Cain answered. Good, just like the plan, he's the only one that knows how to unlock the door, and they sent him off into another world just like Baal. We are all lost. "If you trade the human's freedom for your own, then he could free you," Cain said. Gadreel looked down at Cain before turning to the mirror. "I'm guessing the human knows the way out?" Gadreel asked. Cain said nothing to him but nodded. He turned to the door and then back to Cain. "Very well, then," Gadreel grumbled. Before Cain could say anything, a glow filled the mirror, and before Cain knew it filled the room.

I now had the glowing sword held out in front of us, but there was just one problem. I couldn't get it to do anything. "Well, human, anytime now?" Baal boomed. "I don't know how to make it go," I answered back. Baal human head rolled its eyes at me. "It's like having the Creator in your hand. Just think about the outside of the mirror. That and only that," Baal boomed. I closed my eyes, and I could feel the warm light, unlike anything I felt before. I opened my eyes and saw a circle-like window, and there was everyone. Cain, Gadreel, and his fallen friends. "You ready?" I asked looking over at Baal. "Human, I have been ready for one hundred years," he boomed. I held the sword high in the air and brought it down on the window. I was blinded by white light, and then there was nothing.

A white light filled the room, and a loud boom followed. Cain opened his eyes to see me standing there with Baal towering over him. "Nice plan, Freddie," Cain muttered under his breath as Gadreel and Azazel had looks of shock on their faces. "At last! In the name of the Creator, I will destroy you fallen scums!" Baal boomed. I ran over to Cain and pulled him to his feet. "We better find a way out of here. I have a feeling that Baal will bring the house down," I said as the floor shook. We both looked over to see Baal doing battle with the Fallens. Azazel was on the floor trying to stand as Baal stomp away on him. All around us, the room's stone bricks started to crack. "Shit, he's ruining everything!" I shouted. I looked over to the door. "I hope you have a way out of here, Freddie?" Cain asked, looking over at me. "I didn't think that far ahead," I answered. We ran to the door as part of the wall on the right side fell on the floor. "Let's hope this works," Cain said. Cain pulled out the key that I got from the woman and put it into the door's lock. A boom filled the room as Gadreel was knocked into one of the pillars to our left. "Let's get the hell out of here!" I snapped. We ran through the door and down the hallway. "We got to get to the courtyard!" Cain shouted. A large stone dropped in front of us, and we quickly jumped over it. We could hear bits of yelling from the room. "Damn you, demon fool. Lookout!" Cain saw the doorway light filled our faces as we came out, waiting, there was that woman that took us to the room. "We freed your boyfriend. And we better get out of here before we go down with the ship," I yelled. The woman waved us along, and with her, in the lead, she led us to the large door that we walked into about an hour ago. We ran out of the giant golden castle and onto a blacktop road. "What the hell is this a road?" I asked. "You don't have roads in your world?" Cain questioned back. "We have and it looks just like the roads there," I answered. "Must have been a demon who have built your roads," Cain said. We were about halfway down the road when a red beam of light filled the sky. I could see Gadreel, Azazel, and Asbeel in the sky with Baal firing red beams at each other. "Keep moving!" the woman shouted, taking off again. Both I and Cain followed her on the road until it dead-ended into the woods. "We need a way off this island," I said. The woods opened up to the sand and water in front of us. "Well, I'm fresh out of ideas," I said, looking back at the castle as part of it fell on the ground. I stepped out into the water, and a large head came from the water. "Behemoth," I said. "I see you and the human have caused more damage," it said, floating over to us. "Hurry, all of you. I don't think they will be happy when they get free from Baal," Behemoth said. We hopped on its head, and Behemoth swims away as fast as it could, as what was left of the castle fell on the ground.

Sheol & Astaroth

Behemoth came to rest on a piece of ice that was resting on what looked like a beach. "Where are we?" I asked. "Sheol, I hope you have something to keep you warm," Cain said as we hopped off Behemoth. "I hope the best to you both," it said, disappearing into the water. "She...he...whatever, is very nice. It?" I muttered. "Behemoth is an odd one but yes, Behemoth is nice," Cain smiled. I felt like a bit of an ass while Cain looked up to the mountain that loomed in the distance. "We have to go there, Freddie," Cain pointed to the mountain. "Damn, that's a long way," I said. "I know, so we better get moving now," Cain said, walking off the beach. I followed close behind as we walked through ice-covered leaves. "How cold does it get around here?" I asked. "You don't want to know," Cain answered. Cain stopped suddenly at the bottom of a hill. "Cain, what's going on?" I asked. "Seem like one of your friends has arrived," Cain answered, pointing to the top of the hill. Michael came, covered in a brown-colored cloak. "Well, we couldn't have used you back at the castle," I said. "I'm sorry that I was not there, but I had a feeling that you could handle them," Michael said. He held out his hand to help me up, pulling me to the top. Once we were together at the top, I looked out to see a large chain coming from the top of the mountain. "Why is there a chain coming out of that mountain?" I asked. "That is where Lucifer is. The chain keeps him in hell so that he doesn't get free," Michael answered. "I'm guessing the hole is there too?" I questioned. "Yes, for you to return, you must cut the chain and free Lucifer," Michael answered. "Great, and you're telling me this now. Don't you think you should have told me before we started!" I snapped. "Easy, friend. Michael is just trying to get you there, get you home," Cain said, resting a hand on my shoulder. I turned away from Michael and looked out to the mountain. "I have a feeling that there's going to be a little family get together once we get there," I muttered.

Gadreel was knocked into what was left of the castle as Azazel attack Baal. Once again, he was outsmarted by the human, Asbeel and Penemue tried to attack as well. "That damn human will pay for this with his life," Gadreel breathed. Baal had managed to fight them back to the water edge, and with Baal now at full power, he used his bow. It's been almost five hundred years since he last used it but the time is not yet right. Gadreel put his hand up to the red sky, and a lightning bolt hit his hand. He pointed it at Baal, who was battling Azazel, and pulled the bolt back, and a second lightning bolt appeared. Baal turned to see it and looked up to Gadreel, and ran at him as Gadreel let the bolt go. The lightning bolt shot through the air, hitting Baal's toad head and blasting it to pieces. Baal fell to the ground and he stopped moving. "Gadreel, you called down your bow," Penemue said. "Yes, to kill a demon and to put a human in his grave," Gadreel murmured.

Michael was right, it was cold, and it was unlike anything I felt before. If Afghanistan was cold, this place took the cake. "Damn, who turned the freezer on?" I asked. "It will only get colder. The mountains here are the coldest place in hell it would freeze a human within seconds," Michael said. "Note to self, don't wear shorts here," I muttered. Michael took a step and stopped suddenly, looking back across the water. "Michael, buddy, are you okay?" I asked. Michael's face suddenly looked pale white as he turned back at me. "We need to get you out of here," Michael muttered. Cain had a puzzled looked on his face as Michael started walking again, almost at a powerwalk-like pace. Something scared him, I thought nothing scares these guys. I guess I was wrong.

Nimrod was still waiting for me and my guides to arrive. He managed to take the back way to the hole. And was now waiting for me to show up. "This human must better hurry otherwise I'm going to freeze to death before he gets here," Nimrod said. His army was placed all around the mountains and would see us arrive. He told them not to stop us but allow us to enter the mountain to trap us inside. "I just hope these damn fools don't get spotted," Nimrod breathed. The air was cold and would freeze anything wet. The only thing that was saving my human body from freezing was my armor which kept me warm even in Gehenna. Nimrod looked up to a large winged man frozen, and held one of the Princes of Hell known as Lucifer in his prison.

It could be Gadreel had called down the lightning down and now has his bow back. Getting me to Gehenna was needed more than ever. We needed to get to the hole first and drop me into it, sending me back to Earth. Michael will have to tell me about my father and what I was meant to do in hell. He thought that I might get mad about it, but it's the only way. Michael can only hope that I will take it well. "Freddie, I need to ask you something," Michael said. "What?" I questioned back. "Your father, tell me what you know about him," Michael asked. Freddie looked up at the sky before answering. "My mother told me that he was an okay guy. He would hit her from time to time, but that changed one day after an accident he got into, why?" I asked. "I must tell you about your real father," Michael said, stopping in front of both Cain and me. "I think I know what you're going to say, that my father is down here somewhere, right?" Freddie said. "You could say that, but your real father is someone I know like the back of my hand," Michael said. My face didn't give anything to what he just said. "Your father is my brother," Michael muttered, looking away from me. Cain looked over at me. "Your brother, and who is your brother? Don't tell me it's Gadreel. Damn it, I knew it!" I snapped. I smiled at him. "No, not Gadreel, someone more powerful than him," Michael answered. "Who is more powerful than Gadreel and those demons?" I asked. "I want you to hear it from someone that was there the day you were born," Michael answered. "And who is that?" I questioned. "He would be your uncle and the Crowned Prince of Hell, Astaroth," Michael replied. The color in my face drained away. "Great, so, my old man is the boss down here. Well, so much for going to church every Sunday," I breathed. Michael looked over at me to see that I was looking down at the ground. "What's wrong, friend?" Michael asked. "What am I?" I questioned back. "I want you to talk with your uncle, then you will know everything," Michael answered. "You mean everything you already knew?" I asked. "Yes, it's true. I know a great deal about you, I just didn't believe that you would come," Michael explained. Cain looked over at Michael and then at me. "So, you knew why this human is in hell, and you never told him yet?" Cain questioned. "Yes, I didn't know that this is the final hour," Michael answered. Michael looked over to me, not saying a word. "What do you mean the final hour?" I asked. "By you coming to us, it means that the end of time has come to men, and you will be the one to bring it by freeing the Princes of Hell," Michael answered. I looked over to him, not saying a word. "We need to talk better about this later, once we are safe," Cain muttered. I looked away from Michael and followed Cain as Michael walked behind us, wondering if it was a good idea to tell him about all of this.

Great, not only have I been lied to in my world. I found out that I'm the son of a fucking demon. I might as well burn down a church and just punch my ticket to hell. I only hope that there was a good reason for not telling me about it. Before I could yell at Michael, Cain said that we had to move out. I walked behind him, not saying a word as Michael walked behind us. Cain walked down the frozen path and looked up to the sky. Somewhere under the red sky, my father was watching or waiting for me. "Tell me, Michael, why can't you tell me that I am the *end* before we started this fucking walk!" I shouted. Michael walked up to me, stopping right in front of me. "I didn't know that the human before me was the one that was foretold to bring about the end. Plus, the Creator has lost all hope in the human race, and nothing that we tell him can change his mind," Michael answered. "Freddie, you have nothing to be mad about. What Michael tells you is the truth," Cain said. I looked over at him. "How do I know that? I'm just some kid from North Carolina!" I snapped. "I can read any mind in hell since I was sent here for killing my brother, But you…I can't read yours," Cain muttered. I looked over to him. "I don't get it, what does that mean?" I asked. "It means that you are a part-angel from someone in your family," Cain answered. "Well, my mother was a church person, could have got it from her," I said. "For me to not be able to read your mind takes an angel power, unlike anything I've known," Cain said. "You're meant for something better. The Creator has been known to put people like that to the front of any line," Cain added. I said nothing to this as Michael spoke. "We didn't want to tell you about what we heard from the Creator, but you are the one we have been waiting for. The one who will bring about a new world from the ashes of the old," Michael said. "Thanks, but I don't know if I need to celebrate or what after hearing all these things," I said. "We need to get somewhere we can talk about this, and unlike you two, I need sleep," Cain said. I looked over to him and saw that he had bags under his eyes and some color on left his face. I think it was because he was hanging out with the guy who will help destroy the world. We walked for a while with nothing to say to anyone. I thought about my mother and if she knew her little boy is half-demon or just weird. Cain found a large cave just off the small trail, and he fell asleep soon after we settled. "I wish I could sleep like that," I muttered. Michael said nothing, I felt like that maybe I was too hard on him. "Freddie, there is something I must tell you," Michael said. I looked over at him. "I think you've told me enough," I smiled. "No, not yet. The Creator lost faith in you humans, he told me to do something that I don't agree with," Michael muttered. I said nothing to the feeling. Another bombshell was about to drop on me. "I was sent here to kill you," Michael said. I nearly fell to the ground, that wasn't a bombshell, more like an atomic bomb. "God wanted to kill me?" I breathed. "Then I'm glad you didn't do it," I added. "When the Creator told us to love you, humans, before him, I was the first who showed support. I watched as you grew, and with time, you humans became great. You still fight over race and religion, but you have a strength that can't be measured," Michael said, looking me in the eyes the whole time. "Then what is it you want me to do?" I asked. "Be a human. Be an idea," Michael answered.

 Gadreel stood on the water edge, looking off into Sheol. "Gadreel, we'll be unable to fly for long periods here," Asbeel said. "I'm not worried. He'll have to go to the hole, and Nimrod will be waiting for him," Gadreel said. "Hopefully, that fool can handle it until we show up," Penemue said. "If he can't, then I will make him wish he had," Gadreel smiled. The green color of his eyes became an evil hazel.

 Cain woke up shaking. I feared from the moment we got into Sheol that I should have left him somewhere safe while I am perfectly okay, because of the powers I gained. "Freddie, are you okay?" Cain asked. "Good, just found out that everything in my life is a game, but other than that, I'm good," I answered. Cain let out a cough-like laugh as he looked over at us. "Well, I'm glad you can still make jokes, Freddie," he said. We started walking the trail over a frozen lake, and that's when we walked upon a body, and not just anybody. "What the hell is this, Michael?" I asked. "This is a fallen angel, held here until the end of time," Michael answered. "So, this place is like a prison?" I asked again. "Yes, for my brothers and sisters that went against the Creator," Michael answered. I looked out, and Michael followed my glaze to the other bodies that were lying just ahead of us. "Can they see us?" I asked. "No, but they can hear us," Michael answered. "Just as long as they don't break out and try to kill us," Cain said. "Your joking, right? I mean, they can't wake up, can they?" I asked with a look of worry on my face. "No, I don't think so," Michael answered. "You don't know? I guess you were out when they had the planning of this," I muttered. "Most of these brothers and sisters are older. Some of them have been here since the beginning," Michael said. The ground was white in color and the clouds above us were blocking out the red sky. "What is that?" I pointed to the base of the mountain. Michael looked over and saw a sister, but she looked like she saw better days. Most of her face was missing and lying frozen at her feet. "Damn, who the hell did this? It looks like someone broke her skull open," Cain coughed. I gave Cain some water as I looked at her. "One of the Fallens. It must have been Astaroth," Michael said. "Where is he at?" I asked. Michael looked to the base of the mountain and pointed that way. "He's there, the only Prince of Hell not to be taken," Michael answered. "I'm guessing they stayed clear of this guy because of this," I pointed to the broken face of Michael's sister. "He can do much worst, my friend," Michael said, pointing up his head to the next group of bodies that were damaged in almost the same way. The only difference was that some of the bodies were missing arms, and their wings were smashed off. "Has anyone told him that he might need a hobby?" I muttered. "Come, we must go and see him," Michael said, walking on. "Cain, you're not looking too hot man, you got something hanging for your nose," I said. "Well, unlike you two, I'm still somewhat human, this cold is bad for me," Cain stuttered. "Is there a place where he can warm up?" I asked. "The home of Astaroth should be hot," Michael answered. "Good, we get him warm, and then we get to the bottom of this whole thing," I said, walking ahead.

The angel graveyard gave me the creeps. Most of them had their faces smashed off, or arms and wings have broken off. Just ahead of us was a large house that was looking back at us from the clouds. Suddenly, Michael stopped, and Cain grabbed hold of my hand. "What's wrong?" I asked, looking around. "He's here," Michael muttered. Before I could ask, the ground shook, and I fell to my knees. Michael stepped in front of us as a cloud started to move in like a blanket. "Well, well, what is this that comes my way?" the voice whispered. "Michael, don't tell me you're here for your brothers and sisters. I'm sorry, but they won't be much use to you now," the voice added. "Astaroth, we would like to talk with you!" Michael shouted. The ground shook a few more times, and out from the clouds came a figure about five-ten feet tall with angry-looking red eyes. "Well, at least he looks human," I whispered to Michael. "What is it you want, Michael, and do not make me ask again?" Astaroth questioned. "We need to talk with you about your younger brother," Michael said before Astaroth cut him off. "I do not care for my brother, and you angel shouldn't be asking about a man that is a frozen block of ice," Astaroth snapped. Astaroth stepped forward and started to sniff the air before taking a step forward. "A human, oh, you're his son," Astaroth grinned. I looked over at Michael, and Michael looked back at me, nodding as I stepped forward. "Yes, his son," Michael muttered. "I'm guessing you know nothing about him. Michael, you could have told him about his father too. Both of you use to work together," Astaroth said. "You mean Lucifer!" I shouted. "Yes, human, you would be my kin as well as Michael," Astaroth said. I looked over at Michael, who said nothing as I looked up to Astaroth. "What does the bastard want with me?" Astaroth smiled. "I'm wondering why a demon as powerful as you hasn't tried to run things," I said. Astaroth said nothing as I looked over at Michael. "I think it might be something else. I think you might be scared of Gadreel," I muttered. Astaroth stood straight up and towered over the three of us. "I'm scared of no angel, not Michael, and damn sure not Gadreel," Astaroth snapped. I looked around us before looking back up at him walking up to him. "I think you're scared of him, otherwise, Gadreel would have been killed by now," I said, now standing close to him. He looked down at me. "You are indeed the fool's child. Only Lucifer would dare talk to me that way," Astaroth smiled. I was still a little worried about him, he could smash me flat and think nothing of it. "Follow me, this is no place to be out in the ice talking about your old man," Astaroth said. He turned and walked away with us, following him to the giant castle just off in the distance.

Michael thought that Astaroth would kill me for talking to him like that. I think we got lucky but how long it will hold is anyone's guess. Astaroth walked up the steps to his large door lying on the ground next to a pile of bones. "Take a good look at him, angel. He might be someone you know," Astaroth said. Michael said nothing to it as I looked back at him but said nothing as well. "Well, at least I can feel my hands again," Cain said. Astaroth walked into a large room, and Michael was almost knocked back by how hot it was. "Now human, or should I call you a demon? What is it that you want, boy?" Astaroth asked. I stepped forward. "I want to know how it happened," I answered. "Oh, you want to know how your mother and Lucifer had you. Well, that's a long story," Astaroth answered. "Well, we got a lot of time," Michael said. "About a thousand years ago Lucifer left. Don't ask me how, but he did. Then one day, he looked down into the hole and was never the same after that day. After talking with my brother, whom he didn't like to do, we found out about you. I never thought that I would be face to face with a child of Lucifer. The Creator kills all of them, and so far, you're number six," Astaroth said. "He kept close watch over you, until one day, Gadreel came down to hell after bumping with a human. From what I heard, it was worst than that," Astaroth said. "What do you mean?" Michael asked. "Your brother Gadreel gave birth to evil, to the King of Kings," Astaroth answered. "You are lying, demon," Michael snapped. "Watch your tone with me, angel, bad enough, your kind has given rise to the King of Kings," Astaroth shouted. "Okay, both of you, chill. Now the first question who is this King of Kings?" I asked. "He's known in your world as the Anti-Christ. The one that will rule the world," Cain answered from the chair that he was sitting in. "So, let me understand if I heard this right. Gadreel had a child, and this kid is going to end up destroying the world. Which begs the question, why is Gadreel really after me?" I asked, looking over at Michael. But he said nothing to me, there was nothing to say. "I think I know why," Cain said with a smile.

Both Michael and I looked over at him. I think even Astaroth had a puzzled looked on his face.

I looked at Cain as he stood up and walked over to Michael. "Gadreel has his lightning back and with that, it means that the Creator already gave him the permission to get rid of you," Cain said. "What? The Creator wouldn't let a Fallen kill a human," Michael snapped. "Well, this is fucking funny. So, human, how does it feel knowing that the Creator doesn't care about you?" Astaroth laughed. I would have punched this assclown in the face if it wasn't for the fact that I wanted to know more. "What do you mean he's got his lightning back?" I asked. "An angel can control any of the elements on Earth. When an angel falls, those powers are taken from him forever. Only when the angel believes in the Creator again will those powers return," Michael muttered. "It also means that the angel will be given a task, that will show if he trusts in the Creator," Cain said, looking over at Michael. "And he took up the task that I didn't want to do," Michael muttered. Astaroth's face was like a stone as he turned at me. "Well, human, your trust in the Creator seems to be a waste of time," Astaroth smiled. "Has anyone told you that you're a bit of a dick?" I said. Astaroth's smile seemed to beam more at it. "I could help you boy, but it would cost you something," Astaroth said. "What is it? And if you say something about killing someone, I'm out," I snapped. "No, no, nothing that crazy, human, you must bring me the Ark," Astaroth said. "The Ark? What the hell is that?" I asked. I looked over at Michael, and the color on his face faded like a haze. "The Ark of the Covenant is what held the Ten Commandments that Moses brought down from the mountain," Cain answered. "If you can bring me that, I will help you with your problem," Astaroth said. "Do you know where the Ark of the Covenant is?" Michael questioned. "Yes, angel, but there's a small problem that I just can't get by," Astaroth muttered. "What is it?" I asked. "The Seven Deadly Sins, I can't get past them, but I have a feeling that the son of Lucifer can," Astaroth smiled. There's really something about him I just didn't like, and how come a demon of his power needs help getting this Ark thing anyway. I walked over to Michael, and Cain joined. "I don't like it. I know he's hiding something, and I like to know what," I whispered. Michael nodded and looked over at Cain, I don't know what Michael's plan was, but I hope it wouldn't piss off Astaroth. "You're right, Freddie, he's hiding something, but I can't see it well," Cain whispered. "Fine, I'll get Ark for you!" I shouted. "Good, your father would be proud of you for doing this," Astaroth smiled.

Gadreel was floating high in the sky as Asbeel flew to him. "Gadreel, we might have found the human," he said. Gadreel smiled. "I know where he is, and I even know what that foolish human is going to do," Gadreel said. "What do you mean?" Asbeel asked. "It must be that demon Astaroth. He's always wanted the Ark," Gadreel answered. "But no one can get to it. It's protected by the Seven Deadly Sins," Asbeel muttered. "I know. That's why he will ask the human. Daystar's boy," Gadreel said. "What? Lucifer had a son? Impossible," Asbeel said. "Lucifer did the same thing I did. Mated with a mortal woman and out came his son," Gadreel murmured. "That means he can free his father," Asbeel said. "I don't care about that, you fool. If he gets to the Ark, then everything will change," Gadreel said, grabbing Asbeel by the neck. "We must kill this human, so I can take my place back in the Creator's kingdom and destroy it from within," Gadreel said. Gadreel held his hand up to the sky, and a bolt of lightning hit his hand. "Now the game can begin," Gadreel murmured.

I was walking behind Michael as we crossed a sizeable ice-covered field. "I couldn't get a good read, but I think he might be trying to trick us," Cain said. "I figured as much, I think we might need a plan in case this goes bad," I said. "What are you going to do, Freddie?" Michael asked. I looked up at him. "I don't know, but let me tell you this. We aren't going to give him the Ark," I answered. "Then we better get a plan ready now. If we go back there and give him the Ark, then he might try to get rid of us," Cain said, looking back to both of us. "I need to know what the Seven Deadly Sin is. A monster of some kind?" I asked. "No, not like what you have faced. Whatever sin you have done in the Creator's world is what you will see. This thing is unlike any demon. It can take any shape, even a friend or family member," Michael answered. I looked ahead of us, thinking of something. "I hate to break you away from your moment Freddie, but we need to get moving," Cain said. Michael looked up to see something odd light up in the sky. "Lightning," Michael muttered. Cain and I looked up and saw it too. "What the hell is that?"

I asked. "Whatever it is, we might not want to meet it until after we get the Ark," Cain said, looking at me. "Then we must get moving. Gadreel has his lightning back, and we can't get in a fight with him," Michael said. "I have this funny feeling that I'm the bait in some crazy game," I muttered. "Isn't there a saying on Earth, *he works in mysterious ways*," Cain said. "Well then, let's get it on," Freddie muttered.

Jophiel stood outside his house, and Gabriel and Uriel joined him. "I see you're doing well, brother," Jophiel said. Gabriel rubbed his neck. "Yes, feeling much better thanks, to you and Freddie," Gabriel said with a weak smile. "There will be more work to do soon," Jophiel said. "Brother? Brother, what's wrong?" Uriel asked. "It's Gadreel, he has regained his bow," Jophiel answered. "What? I thought that was impossible!" Gabriel snapped. "Yes, and it was told that none of us would die. I guess that was wrong too," Uriel murmured. "If Gadreel has his bow back, then that means he would have the same power he had when he fell. Now add his fallen powers to that and….," Jophiel muttered. "He would be more powerful. Even more powerful than Michael," Gabriel finished. "We must go and help them," Uriel said. "Yes, but how? None of us can stand up to Gadreel now," Gabriel said. "May I suggest something?" a voice said from behind them. They all turned, and before them was a man dressed in gold and white looking back at them thru an eyeglass. "Brother," Uriel muttered. "It's good to see you, all of you," he said. "Why are you here, does the Creator bring news?" Jophiel asked. "Yes, but it's not for you. The human, Freddie, is who I need to speak to," he answered. "Well, he's out in hell, Malak. What word do you bring?" Jophiel asked, walking up to him. Malak adjusted his glasses before he spoke. "I can't tell you, brother. I'm sorry. I can only talk with the human," Malak answered. "Freddie is in hell trying to get back home. How are you going to find him?" Uriel questioned. "I will only talk with the human, and the human only, sister!" Malak snapped. The three of them said nothing as Malak disappeared in a golden light, leaving the three of them looking up at the red sky.

We stood at the doorsteps of what Michael was telling me was the Seven Deadly Sins. "Okay, got to clear my mind if I'm going to get this Ark back," I said. "Remember, whatever sin you have done in your world will be made real inside," Michael said. I turned away from them and walked up to the door, and it opened with no one on the other side. I looked down what looked like a hallway and looked back at both Michael and Cain. Both gave me a weak smile. "Here goes nothing," I whispered and walked inside. Once inside the building that I couldn't see from the outside, the door closed on me, and I was in darkness. I tried to feel my way around, but that wasn't happening. "Wish I had a light," I said. Suddenly, the light filled the vast space, and standing in front of me was an old woman who needed a visit to a dentist. Most of her teeth were yellow, and some were missing. "Why have you come, human?" she asked. I took a step towards her. "I'm here for the Ark of the Covenant," I answered. The woman looked at me, and I saw that she was missing an eye and the other was a green color. "All who have come to take it have all died," the woman breathed. "Well, that's shit. Thanks, that's good to know," I muttered. "Come, if you think you can take it. Face your fears, human, face them," the woman said. She turned and started walking away. I followed, but not too close, just in case. Even in the darkness, I thought I saw something move to our left. The woman didn't seem to worry about that and keep walking until a tree appeared in the light. "Touch the tree, human, and then we'll see if you can take it," the woman said. I looked over to the woman and then to the tree. "Is this some kind of joke?" I asked. "Touch the tree, and you will begin," the woman answered. I touched the tree, and I felt the air grow heavy, and the darkness starts to take shape. I looked around, and that's when the voices began to talk. It's like being in a room with everyone talking at once. The voices grew louder and louder until I couldn't hear anything else. "What the hell is this?!" I yelled. I fell to my knees and took my hand away from the tree, but this only made things worse. I looked over to the old woman, and she looked back at me with a kind of sad look on her face. I closed my eyes and focus on my breathing, and slowly, the voices started to die down. I opened my eyes, and it was a view that shocked me to my bones.

  I was standing in a frozen city, bodies were spread out on the street. The city was one that I couldn't recall. "Where the hell am I?" I said, looking around. I walked up to a body lying up against a car, it was wearing military body armor, a weapon of M4 was just out of reach. "What is this?" I asked myself. "It's the end of your world, and all things," a voice said. I looked around and saw no one. "Who's there?!" I shouted. "Calm, human, I come with a message from the Creator," the voice answered. "Where are you?" I asked. Just then, I heard ice-crunching footsteps, and a man came into view. He was wearing glasses with a white and gold-colored shirt and pants. "I'm Malak. I believe Jophiel told you about our titles. I would be the Word of the Creator," Malak said, walking up to me. "So, Malak, how can I help you?" I asked. "I wish to give you a message. All of this you see will be the beginning of the end for this world. If you wish the Ark, it will only bring pain to your world," Malak answered. "Whoa, I'm not trying to destroy the world. I'm just trying to get back home," I said. "Then you must send the Ark to your world and not give it to Astaroth," Malak said. "What, you mean all this is because I gave Astaroth the Ark?" I questioned. Malak said nothing but nodded to me as I stepped back, looking up to the white sky of this frozen world. "So, what does God want me to do?" I questioned again. "He wants you to have Michael send it to Earth. The humans will find it and will do what they will with it," Malak answered. "So, I'm guessing you had a talk with the Sins about this. You know how to send this little message" I smiled. "In a way, yes. Take heart, human, you have done what few couldn't," Malak said, turning away from me. "Oh, and what is that?" I asked. "The Creator is watching and waiting for your judgment," Malak answered, walking away. He disappeared into the mist that suddenly started to cover the street. "Well, now that the angel is gone, I can have my fun," a voice said. "You must be the Sins," I said, looking around for something or someone. "Yes, son of Daystar," the voice said. It was like seven or eight people were talking at the same time. "Let the game begin," the voice added.

Michael sat outside the door on the step as Cain looked out into the ice-covered forest. "So, Michael, you haven't told the boy about what he'll have to do," Cain said, looking into the woods. "No, I don't think I would have the stomach to do that," Michael answered. "I think you should tell him. He's strong, but he's still a human, and they are still weak things," Cain muttered. "I believe in them, just like my other brothers that took up this task," Michael said. "Sometimes, truth is the greatest strength anyone can ever have," Cain said. Michael looked up to the red sky before glancing back at the door.

I was knocked to the ground by a half-naked man. Something in me wanted to scream at him to find a pair of pants. His head was mostly bone and some of his flesh fell off. "Greed, greed little bastard," the man kept saying. "Yeah, yeah, you got something else to say other than that?!" I shouted. I jumped behind a burned-out truck as he came running past me, his long black nail was the only color that I could see. "Great, maybe I should have asked about how to get rid of these guys once I meet them," I whispered, running out into the street. The man saw me and came running again. This time, I pulled out the hammer. "I'm going to give you a lesson in a human game called baseball," I muttered. He jumped into the air, and I came across my body with the hammer hitting him square in the head. He went flying into a shop front and breaking the glass. "Dusty fucker" I muttered, putting the hammer away. "Try to take the Ark. Start wanting to make a deal with me. But you, you won't do. Pride….," the voice said. "I don't make deals, I take chances," I said. "Then this will be your last chance," the voice answered back. I looked back to see the man back on his feet. "Prideful…prideful, fool," he said. "Well, at least you're saying something new," I said. The man's arms and legs started to grow until they were at least six feet long. "Maybe instead of chasing me, you should join the basketball team," I muttered, pulling out the hammer. "Prideful, fool," the man said, running at me. I dodged his left hand only to get kicked in the side. He then grabbed me and, in one motion, tossed me away. I got to a knee and looked back to see this man or demon running at me again. When he reached for me, I hit him in the head, knocking him to the ground. I put the hammer high above my head and dropped it right on his head. It was like watching a tube of toothpaste being squeezed empty. A black liquid covered the ground, pooling under his body. "You wish the Ark that bad human?" the voice asked. "Yes, now show yourself!" I answered. Came out a little stronger. I turned to see a naked woman standing there, her dark jet black hair the only thing covering her breast. "Now, do you want to talk about giving me the Ark, or do we have to go through another fight again?" I asked. "I will not give you anything human, or should I say… little Daystar? The Ark must stay in this world," the woman answered. "Oh, why?" I asked. "Because you humans aren't ready for the truth, for His word," the woman replied. "Since when does a demon care about the word of God?" I questioned. "We Sins live off your human sin, and the original sin came from you humans long ago," the woman answered. "So, you live. Wait, are you trying to say….," I stuttered. "Yes, human, if you sent the Ark back to your world, it will start the End of Days for your people," she murmured. "I need it to give it to Astaroth," I breathed. "Even worse, he will destroy it and have full rule over your people!" she shouted. "Well then, you shouldn't be worried," I said. "Fool! Astaroth will go to your world, and his word will be the only word you will know!" she yelled. Two things I hate are one, somebody that likes to yell. Two, being used by people, and this sounds like I'm being used. "Then what do you want me to do about it?" I asked. "Leave, human, and never return to this place," she answered. "I can't do that, woman. I have a fallen angel after me getting him off my case!" I snapped. That was something I never do to people, but I didn't have the time to tell her my life story. "Give me the Ark, demon, or I will kill you," I said, putting the hammer away and pulling out the sword. "I will not let you kill my kind, human," she roared as she started to change. I was looking at a growing monster, sharp teeth began to fill her largemouth. "Okay, come to papa," I whispered.

She had changed into an eight-story monster. She looked like a massive spider with the back end of a snake. Where the spider's eyes were her body's upper half. "Shit just keeps getting better and better all the time," I breathed. It looked down at me. "You will bring the end to us all!" it boomed. "Listen, I just want to go home. I'm not trying to hurt anyone!" I shouted. "Bringer of death, keeper of sin. Why should you be believed?!" it called, as the street shook. It took two massive steps smashing a car as it walked. "Humans are liars, fools all of them," it boomed. As I started to run, the sounds of glass breaking and metal being crushed filled the empty street. I ran down to the end of the road and turned left as it knocked part of the building. Pieces of the building rained down to the street. I jumped through a storefront and rolled to a stop against a freezer. "Damn, I would rather be in a firefight right now than putting up with this shit," I breathed. The floor shook as it walked down the street knocking over cans and bags of chips. "Think, Freddie. Damn, you're better than this," I muttered. I walked to the back door of the shop and kicked the backdoor opened. I could only think of one person who could get me out of this. "Jophiel. Jophiel, it's me, Freddie. I need your help," I said to myself. "Freddie, it's good to hear your voice again," Jophiel said. "I need some help. I'm trying to find the Ark, but I'm dealing with a huge bitch," I said, walking down the alley. "Why are you trying to get the Ark?" Jophiel asked. "Astaroth said that if I get the Ark for him, he would help me. Let me guess, bad idea?" I questioned back. "Yes, very bad idea. I'm guessing you must have found out about your father," Jophiel said. I appeared from the alley and crossed the street into another shop that sold jewelers. "Yes, and you could have told me, but never mind that. I got a guest just before this started by the name of Malak. He told me to have Michael send the Ark to Earth," I said. "Yes, I figured that would happen. Freddie, you have to get the Ark to Michael, he will be able to send it to Earth," Jophiel said. "Is it true that if the Ark returns to Earth, then it will start the End of Days?" I asked. Jophiel was silent for two seconds, too long for my taste, but when he answered, it wasn't good. "Yes, it will start with the rebirth of the Creator's son," Jophiel answered. "Shit, the good old damn if you do, damn if you don't deal. Great," I whispered. "I fear it's worse than that. Everything will be destroyed," Jophiel said. "You keep making this whole thing better and better," I muttered. "I told you from the start that the choices you make will change everything," Jophiel said. "I know, but this is...this is way too big for me," I said. "Then have faith, faith in yourself, and faith in the Creator. He will guide you and keep you safe always," Jophiel said. "Thanks, I know what I need to do. I'm just worried about doing it," I said. "Worry not. Sometimes the need overcomes the want," Jophiel said. I kept thinking that Jophiel would have made a good father to some kid somewhere, the only problem would be that he was an angel and might not have been there. I stood there wondering about my father and what he would do once he saw me. Would he even know me? A loud crash woke me from my daydream, and I looked out the broken window to see it crash into a building. "Come out, human, you can't hide from me," it boomed. "I guess I'll choose damn if you do," I muttered to myself. I watched her, she walked by. "Okay, here goes," I said to myself. I ran out onto the street. "Hey, you bitch!" I shouted. It turned its head at me and knocked part of a building down. "Are you done hiding!" it boomed. The large red eyes looked down at me and started to walk back down the street. I ran, looking up, and I saw a tall building at the end of the road. "Right this way," I muttered.

Some would say that my plan was crazy, but it would work, that was for sure. If I didn't die first. It was hot on my heels as I ran into the door, blasting it to piece. A few seconds later, the whole building was like a tornado. Glass rained down to the floor. "Great!" I shouted, running away. I saw some stairs and took them to the next floor as the monster followed slowly. I wait until I could see it and pulled out my sword, and a big smile came across my face. "Got you, bitch!" I yelled, swinging my sword. The sword looked like it was a mile long in my hand as it cut through part of the building. The blade cut through the top part of her head just above the mouth. It stopped dead in the center of the monster's head. It fell down cracking the floor under the head. That must have been all the building could take, a loud metallic creaking sound filled the air, and the floor above fell on top of the monster. Soon the beast was buried underneath brick, chairs, tables, and maybe the kitchen sink. Blinding white light poured into the room, and with a flash, it was gone, leaving a solid gold box about four feet tall and four feet wide. "Let me guess, Ark of the Covenant?" I said to myself. "Time to get you back home," I said, picking it up over my head with both hands. Everything around me started to disappear, and I was once again back in darkness. "You now have the Ark, good luck to you, human," a voice said as a doorway of light appeared next to me. "Thanks for everything, or nothing," I muttered, walking.

Michael was looking over at Cain when the door opened, and soon after, I walked thru. "You guys missed me?" I asked. Cain smiled as I put the Ark down beside the door. "Michael, I need two flavors. One, we need to make a double of this and everything inside," I said. "What? I thought you are going to give it to him?" Cain questioned. "Change of plans. Two, I need you to send this to Earth," I answered. "Earth? What are you thinking?" Michael asked. "I got a damn plan," I smiled.

wWe dropped the Ark of the Covenant at the feet of Astaroth. "You really are the son of Lucifer, good work, human," Astaroth said. He got up and walked up to it touching it before looking over at us. "Good, I will help you get to where you need to go. If you go outside my home, there's a trail that will take you to the mountain. After that, it will be up to you already," Astaroth smiled. "Good, thank you," I said. "No, human, thank you," Astaroth said. We turned and walked out of Astaroth's home and to the trail. "How long will it take him to figure out that it's fake?" I asked. "He shouldn't, no demon has ever seen the Ark before," Michael answered. "I love it when I get over on somebody, and they have no idea," I laughed. "Well, we still have to get inside the mountain, Freddie. Let's not…what's the saying? *Throw a party just yet,*" Michael said. "That was some quick thinking, but what about the real Ark. Now that it's on Earth, will it be safe?" Cain asked. "I think it will be in good hands," I muttered. "You worry about your world?" Michael questioned. "Well, yes, I have to go back there and live, so I'm a little worry," I answered. "I think you will have more important things to worry about," Cain said, pointing up to the mountain. Michael and I looked up to see the light about halfway up the mountain. "Can you see what that is, Michael?" I asked. "Yes, Nephilims," Michael answered. "I think you were right, Cain. I have others things to worry about," I muttered.

"Gadreel must have sent these Nephilims to block us," Michael whispered. "Looks pretty bad, Michael," I said. "I have a feeling that this will get worst before it gets better," Michael said. "We need to take them out first," I whispered. "That part might be easy once we get close enough," Michael said. Cain came over to us and said nothing but pointed up to the stairs just up ahead. "We're going to need to get closer," Michael whispered. I said nothing but nodded as Cain grabbed a rock and tossed it at the bottom of the stair. The loud thud sound echoes up to the Nephilims. They both hopped up to their feet and looked down to the stairs. Michael stood up and shot his bow twice. Both arrows hit their marks, and both fell to the ground. "Go!" I snapped. The three of us ran up the stairs stopping and fired for a moment before looking around. "How far up do these stairs go?" I asked. Michael pointed up higher to the middle of the mountain. "Once we're there, we would have to cross a long bridge into Gehenna and then home," Michael said. "If I had a drink, I would have one to you, sir," I said. Michael smiled at me as we started up the stairs to Gehenna, the frozen hell.

Year 4:
Frozen wasteland of Gehenna

I looked out onto the frozen ground and saw all around us fallen angels. "Wow, how many angels sided with my old man?" I asked. "I'm not sure, but most of them were put in Gehenna. Most of them are here because they mated with human women and made many of the Nephilims that we have run into," Michael answered. "So, how come I didn't join them?" I questioned. Michael stopped and looked back at me. "Your father made sure that you stayed out of the Creator's sight. I don't know how he did it, but he did. That much is sure," Michael answered. I said nothing to it and kept walking. We had run into three more groups of Nephilims coming down the mountain. Strong but dumber than a bag of hair, we had pasted a group of frozen angels with painful looks on their faces. "I don't want to meet what did this," I muttered. "Samuel," Cain said, pointing out ahead of us. Standing there was a man dressed in black holding a sword, I didn't see him when I looked ahead of us a second ago. It was as if he was waiting for someone or something. "I really don't like this, Michael," I whispered. "Brother, what are you doing here?" Michael asked. The angel was different from Michael and the others. First off, his eyes were huge, about the size of a softball, and looked like snake eyes with a yellow tint. "This guy gives me the creeps," I whispered to Cain. "You're looking at Samuel, the angel who was watching over this place," Cain whispered back. Michael walked over to him, touching his shoulder. "Brother, you shouldn't be here, they're coming," Samuel said. "Michael, what's he talking about?" I questioned. Michael looked up to the sky and saw something he didn't like. I looked over to one of the angel bodies and saw that one had its upper half bite off. "I would hate to run into whatever did this," I muttered. Michael turned to us with a look of worry on his face. "We might have some trouble ahead, be ready!" Michael snapped. Cain looked over at me, and I looked back at him. "Okay, don't make us wait, what the hell are we dealing with?" I asked. "Storm of the soulless," Michael answered. "Why couldn't it be hail instead," I muttered to myself. "This is no joke, Freddie. The monsters that live in the storm will kill us all," Michael whispered. Samuel stepped forward. "I will try to keep them busy, but you must hurry," Samuel said. "Thank you, brother," Michael said. A line of black clouds was coming right at us. I could only wonder what could be inside that cloud.

Michael has never seen the Storm of the Soulless before, the only one to ever see it was Gabriel. I took out my sword, and Cain stood ready, as the storm came over us, covering everything around us in darkness. "So, this might be the wrong question to ask, but, what's inside the clouds?" I asked. "Monsters…monsters that used to live on Earth, but were sent here until the End of Days to retake the Earth from humans," Michael answered. "I shouldn't have asked, I knew it," I muttered. "I can't see shit!" I added. Michael put his hand on what he thought was my mouth and only found my forehead instead. "Something is coming," Michael whispered. Cain stayed quiet as Michael looked over at Samuel. Michael moved his hand from my head as we took a step forward. I lost my footing and fell to the ground. "Damn," I murmured. Suddenly, a bright white light appeared in front of me. "What is this?!" I snapped, covering my eyes. "Lookout!" Samuel shouted, pushing me out of the way.

The light blinded me, and I heard Samuel shouted, looking out at me, but I just couldn't see anything. I felt a gust of wind as Samuel, and I fell to the ground. "What the fuck is that?!" I snapped. I let my eyes adjust to the darkness and saw the outline of something large. "What the fuck is that?!" I asked. "One of the many fishes that haven't been in your world since the beginning," Samuel whispered. The fish, if you could call it, was as big as a building and looked like a huge Angler. I stood up and barely made out while Samuel was standing next to me. "How do they hunt?" I questioned. "These monsters use their light to blind the victim before they eat them, or trick them into getting too close and killing them. These monsters live in the cloud eating Nephilims and other fallen angels," Samuel answered. "Great, but that still doesn't answer the question of how a big ass fish lives in a cloud," I said. "To answer that question would take time, human, a time we don't have," Samuel said. "Good point. Like Star Wars and Superman, you don't ask any questions," I muttered. Another light appeared far off to the left, and before I knew it, there were at least twenty lights around us. "Oh shit, this is a problem," I said. Samuel's outline was running now, and as my eyes adjusted to the darkness again, I could see another outline running up to me. "This way quickly!" Cain snapped. I followed, and before I knew it, I was back with Michael and Samuel. "How do we get out of here?" I asked. "There is only one way out, it's at the center of the storm," Samuel answered. "Okay, and how far is that?" I questioned. "The storm is a part of a larger storm, like a hurricane. Only thousands of times bigger than any storm," Michael answered. "I knew I shouldn't have asked that question," I muttered.

Earlier, Michael managed to find Samuel in the darkness, it was unusual darkness. Michael soon met up with Cain and me, and the four of us now huddled close together. "This doesn't look good," I whispered. "There's always a way out, human," Samuel murmured. Ten of the lights followed us and stop floating around us like a ghost. "Run or fight, we're a little outnumbered!" Michael snapped. "Then we run!" Samuel shouted, taking off. We followed behind him, and the lights followed us. As we ran, I could feel the ground move beneath us. "Great, a damn earthquake!" I shouted. Suddenly, the ground opened up from under us, and we fell. Michael opened his wings, and golden light filled the hold as Samuel was floating. In his arms were Cain and me. "I have them, brother" he whispered. Michael floated over to him and took me into his arms. "Listen, first, you better take me out to a movie before I give you anything," I smiled. Samuel looked at me with his puzzled look. "Human sarcasm, brother," Michael said. "I hate to break up the love here, but where the hell are we?" Cain asked. "Hell, duh," I laughed. "I think your human is broken," Samuel said. "No, he's fine. Cain, I couldn't tell you where we are," Michael answered. "We could float to the bottom. Look for a way out," Samuel said. Michael nodded as we floated down, I saw what looked like the bottom and hovered just above it. "Any takers?" Michael questioned. "I guess I'll take a look and see," I said, hopping onto the ground. "Hey, it's solid and warm," I said. Samuel had a troubled look on his face. "I think I know where we are," Samuel muttered. "Okay, but if he says some crazy shit, I'll throw my shoes at him," I said. "We have fallen into the belly of the Evil worm," Samuel said. "Oh, shit, we got eaten?!" I shouted. "No, but we can use this to get to the other side of the storm," Samuel said. "Well, that works for me. As long as there's nothing down here that can beat us," I said. "No, but we might find half-dead fallen angels," Samuel said. "Good, I can deal with that" I smiled. "No, half-dead fallen is much worse than you think," Michael said. "Well, which way do we go? I want to get out of here as soon as possible," Cain said. I pointed into the darkness. "I'm guessing we go that way," I said. "Then we head out into the unknown," Samuel said.

The worm ate just about anything it came across, bones and pieces of stone littered the surfaces. "Michael, how long is this thing?" I asked. "About hundred feet long, more or less," Michael answered with a smile. "Oh, I see," I said. Samuel suddenly stopped and pointed ahead of us. "Something is coming," he whispered. I looked down the tunnel and couldn't see a damn thing, so I had to trust Samuel. "What could it be?" I asked. Michael said nothing. "Whatever it is, it can't be good," Cain whispered. A shape started to form just in front of us. "What is that?" I asked. It was barely visible, but I saw it through the darkness. It had six heads, and they all looked human with large black eyes. The body was like a dinosaur, but at the end of its tail were two more heads. "What the hell is that?!" I snapped. "The first humans, the Creator must have put them in here," Samuel said. "Wait, the first humans, you mean before us?" I asked. "Yes, before Adam and Eve, there was that," Samuel answered, pointing to the monster. "Okay, why would God the Creator make something like that?" I questioned back. "He was trying to make you human," a voice answered. I slowly turned my head to the monster, and one of the heads must have said something. "Did it just talk?" I asked. "Yes, you damn human," it muttered. "What is it you want? Get out of our way, monster!" Samuel snapped. He must have learned that from Jophiel. "I have a feeling that this thing isn't going to move if you keep trying to sweet talk it," I whispered. Samuel looked over at me before looking up at the monster. "Two humans, it has been a long time since I saw a human," it said, stopping in front of us. "Wait, isn't there more of them around here?" I whispered to Michael. "Yes, but my guess is that this one ate all of them," Michael said. I looked up at the monster as smiles spread across each of its faces. "Yes, I did, and now I will add two humans and two angels to my list," all the voices said. "Great, I see why God got rid of you!" I shouted. The monster's heads came down fast and tried to bite us, Michael punched one head away while Cain almost had his arm bit off. "How do we get rid of this thing?!" I yelled. Samuel rolled out of the way and fired a bolt of lightning from his bow. The lightning hit the side of one of the necks and sent pieces of hot meat raining to the ground. "Damn, nice shot!" I shouted. Michael soon followed, and the monster lost three heads. The beast was crying in pain as both Samuel and Michael floated over him. "Leave now while you still can," Samuel said. The monster turned and ran back into the darkness but I could still hear its cries.

Gadreel was standing next to a dead Nephilim when Azazel floated down to him. "Did you see them?" Gadreel asked. "No, unless they went into the storm," Azazel answered. "No, they would be too stupid to do that, very well then, we'll wait for them at the prison of Lucifer," Gadreel said. "Are you sure that's wise, what if they will wake him up?" Penemue asked. "Then, we'll have to take that chance, but that human will not leave hell alive," Gadreel answered. "Go to Nimrod and tell him to get ready for company," Gadreel added. Penemue floated off into the red sky and flew away. "It's been a long time since I got into a good fight," Gadreel laughed.

We walked for what felt like days until we came to a dead end. "Great, now what?" I asked. "Now we cut our way out," Michael answered. He pointed his bow above us and pulled it back. A crack sound filled the air, and the lightning appeared. "Wow, can I get a bow that shoots lightning?" I asked. "You have to work for the man," Michael smiled, letting the lightning fly. It hit the roof, and light soon filled the darkness. "I do work for the man," I paused. "Where are we?" I asked. "You'll find out soon," Michael answered. I smiled at this as Samuel picked up Cain, and Michael picked me up off the ground. We flew into the air and landed next to a frozen tree. "This looks familiar," I said. Michael looked over and saw that the mountain now towered over us. "Damn, we got to go up that?" I asked. "No," Michael said. "Good, so where do we go?" I questioned. "Inside," Michael whispered. I looked at Michael. "All we need now is a ring to throw into the lava," I said. "What?!" Michael asked. "Nothing," Freddie muttered.

I guess that Michael's time with us humans didn't include watching movies. "So, can you tell me about my father?" I asked. Michael looked over at me. "I'm what you would call the younger brother, if you want to know about your father, you should ask Samuel," Michael answered. I looked over at Samuel, who looked back at me with a raised eyebrow. "I see, so, you are his son. Damn. What's the word? *Smartass*," Samuel smiled. I said nothing to it, I couldn't, really. I didn't think I would have that in common with a man, an angel, a demon, whatever the hell he is. "Yes, human, I knew your father. When he was young, and your world was the same. Back then, the Creator told us to put you first above everything, but your father said no. He thought that the Creator should be first in all things, the Creator didn't like it and cast him out from His kingdom," Samuel said. "Sound like he had good reason, you've seen it down there. Killing, war, mass genocide, sounds like we let God down," I muttered. Samuel stopped walking and faced me. "You bring up good points, but you must understand that our job is not to judge you. Our job is to keep you safe without getting too involved," Samuel said. "What do you mean by…too involved?" I asked. "The Creator wanted us to just watch you. If something happened that would destroy the world, then and only then would we act," Michael answered. "Sounds like you guys are very powerful cops," I said. "Cops, what is that?" Samuel asked. "They protect the humans like we do, brother," Michael said with a small smile. "I'm guessing he doesn't go down to Earth much," I whispered. "No, but Samuel knows much of this part of hell," Michael smiled. "I guess that will do," I said. We walked up to a large opening and saw nothing but darkness. "Do you know what could be living in here?" I asked, looking over at Samuel. "Not sure, could be anything," Samuel answered. "I thought you knew much of these parts!" I snapped. A smile soon creeps across his face. "Now wait, wait one damn minute. You know about jokes, but you don't about movies?" I said. Samuel said nothing but gave the universal sign for I don't know, dirty bastard. "This is as far as I can go. Go forth, son of Lucifer, and meet your fate," Samuel said. "Well, I'll catch you later, friend," I said. Michael said nothing but nodded to him as he floated up into the sky. A light was covering him, and soon he disappeared into the clouds. "Michael, can I really save the world? You know, make him change his mind," I asked, pointing up to the sky. "I have a strong feeling that you can, but you must believe, in Him and in yourself," Michael answered.

Michael could sense that I am worried, but my worry was more about meeting my father. Just at the end of the tunnel was his brother, the one he loved and the one that he put down in hell. Cain stood next to Michael. "Are you okay, Michael?" Cain asked. "What? Oh, yes. Just thinking about something," Michael answered. I stepped into the tunnel first. "Well, now or never, folks," I said. We walked into the tunnel, and along the way, we saw Michael's fallen brothers and sisters. "From the looks of this, there must have been a huge battle," Cain said. "Yes, my guess is that Gadreel must have gained the upper hand," Michael reported. Michael sniffed the air and smelled something that came on the breeze. "Nephilims," Michael seethed. "They got here first, fuck, this is a problem," I said, looking back at Michael. "We can't turn back now. We have to get you out of here," Cain whispered. "If there are only Nephilims here, then I can take care of them for you and buy you some time so you can get to the hole, we'll need to free your father to get it open," Michael said. "I can't leave you both to deal with this!" I snapped. "The whole world is hanging on you and this plan. You have to go and don't worry about us. Nothing truly dies in the Creator's world," Cain said. "I will take them. You two will have to free Lucifer," Michael said. I looked over at Cain. "You ready?" I asked. "Are you?" Cain questioned back. The three of us walked down the tunnel to the last test...the Last Judgement.

Cain and I kept close as Michael stepped out into the opening. I could see that most of the Nephilims were spread out inside the ample large space. When I mean big, like Yankee ballpark big. At the center of this was a monster chained up like Mammon, but this thing was way more significant. The face was covered by some kind of mask, and the chains ran from its arms, legs, and wings. The chains met and six places around the room. Michael walked out until four Nephilims saw him and started to shout to the others. "Hurry, get the chains off of Lucifer!" Michael snapped. I ran out of the hiding place at the mouth of the tunnel and ran to the close tie-down point. Cain did the same as Michael flatten one of the Nephilims into a large group of twenty. I got to the first tie-down and saw a sun symbol, with its cut in half with the bottom half darker than the top. "Morning Star, right," I muttered to myself. I pulled out my sword and cut it into the chain, splitting it in half. I saw Cain break the chain loosely with something that looked like a crowbar. As we ran to the following tie-downs, the mountain started to shake, and something crash through the mountain and into the ground. "Whoa, that can't be good," I said. Standing there was Gadreel, and he was soon joined by the rest of his gang. "Shit, *Murphy*, I hate your damn guts," I said. "Michael, brother, it's good to see you," Gadreel smiled. He looked different, dressed in a gold color breastplate, and his wings changed color from black to white. "I guess he had the chance to change clothes," I said. I see you brought the human with you, good. I will do what you couldn't and kill this human," Gadreel said, looking over at me. Michael put his hand up to the hole in the mountain, and the sound of thunder filled the cave. Suddenly, standing next to Michael was Jophiel and the rest of the angel bunch. "Timing is everything," Michael said. "Yes, it is, good to see you, Jophiel," Gadreel muttered. "Go, Freddie, hurry! Return to the human world, now! Be the man you were meant to be!" Jophiel shouted. "Get the human! Bring me his head!" Gadreel snapped. "Well, I always love running for my life," I muttered.

I moved quickly out of sight as Azazel floated up into the air. "Human, come out. Hiding only proves that you're a coward!" Azazel snapped. Gabriel took to the air as he knocked Azazel into the side of the mountain. Gadreel put his hands up to the sky, and the sound of thunder filled the air. "Michael, you know you can't stand me," Gadreel smiled. "I will stand against you until the end," Michael said. "Good, your end is now!" Gadreel shouted, rushing me. Michael was knocked off his feet as Gadreel hit him in the face. But Michael managed to kick him off and blasted him with a wave of fire from his mouth. "Ahhhh…

damn you!" Gadreel snapped. He kicked Gadreel again in the leg, dropping him to his knee. From the tunnel came Nephilims, hundreds of them pouring in. Uriel and Raphael were busy with both Asbeel and Penemue. From above came Jophiel crashing into the ground, sending rock and Nephilim bodies into the air. "Brother, you must mind your surrounding," Gadreel said, stabbing Michael in the back. Michael dropped to his knees, and Gadreel stood up. "Must be my lucky day," Gadreel muttered. Michael looked over to see his sliver blade gripped in his hand. "You see, brother? The Creator has given me back the power you took from me," Gadreel said. "Now, brother, you fall," Gadreel said, holding the blade inches from Michael's face.

I had managed to break the third tie-down when I looked out to see Michael. He was looking around when Gadreel struck, stabbing Michael in the back. "Shit!" I snapped. I was about to jump down and try to get to Michael when some nailed me in the face knocking me down. I looked up to see Nimrod looking down at me, "Well, human, it's good to see you again," he said, grabbing me by my neck. "I'm…guessing…you're still…mad about…me," I stuttered. "I'm going to kill you human… slowly," Nimrod said. Before I could answer, the ground shook, and a hand came up from the ice knocking Nimrod off me. I coughed and looked up to see the large thing now trying to free itself from the rest of the chains. "Father!" I shouted. The monster turned at me and, with his free hand, pulled the mask from his face. I saw that he had six eyes. All of them focused on me. Everything around us stopped, and it became so quiet that you could hear a pin drop. When it spoke, I was even more surprised. "My son, what are you doing here?" he questioned. "I would like to ask you the same question," I answered. He twisted up into a weird smile. "I better get into something better," he smiled. "Lucifer is free. What have you done, human!" Gadreel snapped. Lucifer, the old man, laughed like a wild man before answering Gadreel. "Brother, you froze me in ice. Now, I'm going to rip your wings off of you," Lucifer said. From where I was standing, it looked like Lucifer was getting smaller. Lucifer floated to the ground and looked over at me. "I have to give you something, Freddie, something I took from you when I left," Lucifer said, touching my head. What happened next was…otherworldly.

I felt a power fill my body. "What is this?!" I asked. "You...my son... the real you," Lucifer said, looking out to Gadreel. I looked into the ice and saw a reflection of me if I could call "it" me. I had something on my head that looked like a halo, but it was like someone cut them in half. My eyes were hazed green with lines running down my arms that were purple in color. I looked over at Nimrod, who was still watching Lucifer. I looked over at the old man. "Go have fun," Lucifer smiled, pointing to Nimrod. I walked over to him, and every step I took broke the frozen ground under my feet. "Damn, human!" Nimrod shouted, running at me. I blocked his punch and kicked him in the stomach, sending him crashing into Gadreel. "Well, Gadreel, looks like your kin has come for you," Lucifer laughed. Gadreel tossed Nimrod to the side and stood up. "Well, human, I'm glad you now have power. You're still nothing but a human, an ant to me," Gadreel said. "Come say that to my face, uncle" I smiled. Yeah, he didn't like that much and came flying at me. My eyes tracked him like an anti-air gun, and with one move, I threw the hammer and hit him, clipping his wing. Lucifer was watching like a father watching his son walk for the first time. Jophiel was at Michael's side and was watching as I stood there waiting for Gadreel.

It was unlike anything they've ever seen before. Jophiel was picking Michael up off the ground as he watched me became what I was meant to be. "Tell me, brother, what did I miss?" Michael asked. "Not much. Freddie is handling Gadreel. Lucifer is free," Jophiel answered. "I don't think he cares about us now," Michael said. I picked up Nimrod. Everyone could only hear bits of screaming from Nimrod as I hit him in the chest. Nimrod went flying against the side of the wall, and a crack sound echoed in the air. Nimrod's body laid still as Gadreel stood up. "You should give up, brother. My boy won't ask you again," Lucifer laughed. "Your boy is a damn bastard like his father!" Gadreel snapped. I smiled at him. "Better a bastard than a dead angel," I smiled and grabbed Gadreel up by the neck. I stabbed him in the stomach and dropped him to the ground. "He's all yours, Jophiel!" I shouted. "Well, boy, you're a better human than I," Lucifer said, snapping his fingers. Suddenly Gadreel burst into flames. "The Creator forgives, but I don't," Lucifer muttered. "The rest of you can go, only because I need to do something. Trying to find you will keep me entertained for a time," Lucifer added. The rest of the fallen and Nephilims ran for the exit as Jophiel helped Michael walk over to me. "Are you okay, man?" I asked. "I think I should be the one to ask you that," Michael answered. "Michael, look at you, a damn mess," Lucifer smiled. Uriel and Raphael stood in front of Michael, sword drawn. A light from behind Lucifer blinded me. "It's time, Freddie, time to go," Michael said. I looked over at Michael and said nothing as I turned to Lucifer.

The light was a hole of some kind. I looked back to Jophiel and Michael before I walked over to Lucifer. Who, was walking over to me. "Son, it looks like you have a plane to catch," Lucifer said. "There are many questions I have for you, but I guess they won't get answered now," I said. "Tell your mother I said *hello*" Lucifer smiled. I looked down into the hole as Lucifer looked over at me, pointing to the spot. "Do I have time to say *bye*?" I asked, looking at Michael and the others. "You keep some strange company, boy. Fine, go ahead," Lucifer answered. "Uriel, Raphael, you guys stay safe. Gabriel, try not to get stabbed again. Jophiel, thanks for the heart," I said. I walked up to Michael. "Thank you, Michael, for telling me who I was and for letting me find out on my own," I added. They all gave me a smile, and I turned back to the hole and jumped in. The light was blinding, and I couldn't see anything.

I fell into the hole, and Jophiel walked over to Lucifer. "You could have returned to earth. Replace the boy, make his life your own," Jophiel said. "Yes, but I'm a father first and foremost, I will always be with him," Lucifer said. "Does this mean, the Earth's end will come very soon, now he's back to the world?" Lucifer questioned. "Yes, it has been prophesized already," Jophiel answered. "Then you know whose horse I'm backing," Lucifer said. "I would expect nothing less from a father," Jophiel whispered.

Ending: The Coming War

"The next thing I knew, I'm was waking up in a hospital," I said. "Damn boy...that story was...as long as hell," grandpa stuttered. "Well, you asked me how I felt," I muttered. "Yes, boy, how you felt, not a story," he said, getting up and walking inside. It's been a month since I woke up in the hospital. It was four years that I was in that coma, and I still felt like everything I went through was real. I stayed with my grandpa until my mother returned from the store, so I shared this story with him. He joined me back holding two beers. "Oh, I forgot. I got to drive back to the hotel!" I snapped. "Then take this...with you...silly ass," he said. I said nothing to it. "Maybe...this journey...you went on...was your way...of waking up. Have you...ever thought about that?" grandpa asked. "Yeah, but it was so real to me, I was with Michael and fighting against fallen angels," I said. "It's getting...late, grandson...you should be heading out," he said. "Are you sure you will be okay?" I asked. "Yes, boy...damn, I'm not...going to have...a crazy party...and shit," he said. "Okay, grandpa, see you in the morning," I said, walking off the porch. I walked to my car, which was brand new thanks to good insurance, and waved to my grandpa goodbye. He waved back as I started my car and drove slowly away. On my way out, I passed a silver BMW M3.

The silver BMW pulled into the driveway of grandpa's house. Grandpa was waiting for the man to show up and hope that I would be going. A man stepped out wearing a black suit with a red tie. "You just missed my grandson. How is everything down in the pit?" grandpa asked. "Good, you left it in good hands. How is he adjusting to this world?" the man questioned back. Richard, my grandfather, smiled. "He told me a story about going to hell and fighting angels and shit," he explained. "You play an old man well, hail Satan," the man said. "Shut up, the boy is still clueless but you made a fine son Lucifer. I like the color of your tie," Richard, or should I say, Satan smiled. "His greatest test will come soon. I hope he will be ready," Lucifer worried. "That boy still has all that power. And power changes man," Satan said. "We'll see about that, old man."

www.ingramcontent.com/pod-product-compliance
Lightning Source LLC
LaVergne TN
LVHW091552060526
838200LV00036B/805